BLIND SCUFFLE

The gun went off once, illuminating the determined glare etched across Clint's features.

Keeping hold of the masked man's wrist, Clint sent one of his knees straight up into the guy's stomach. Although he heard a pained grunt from behind the mask, Clint felt like he'd just kicked a tree stump. Pain spiked through his leg, and Clint felt himself being pulled off his feet as the man in front of him tried to reclaim his arm.

"Hold on, Adams!" Ed shouted as he worked his way to where Clint was struggling. "I'm almost there."

Clint felt the arm he was dangling start to swing in Ed's direction. As much as he tried to stop it, Clint knew he wouldn't be able to do anything of the sort with just the grip he had around the man's wrist.

The man with whom Clint had chosen to tangle wasn't much taller than he was, but he seemed to have been built from nothing less than bricks and mortar. No matter how much Clint tried to divert the man's gun hand or shove the guy off balance, he couldn't seem to uproot the attacker.

Finally, Clint stopped trying to chop down the mountain and took a different approach. The seconds had been dragging by and he was afraid he was out of time before the trigger was pulled. Clint didn't have to be looking down the barrel of the other man's gun to know that Ed was about to get himself shot at any moment.

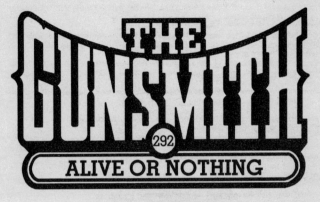

THE GUNSMITH

292

ALIVE OR NOTHING

J. R. ROBERTS

JOVE BOOKS, NEW YORK

THE BERKLEY PUBLISHING GROUP
Published by the Penguin Group
Penguin Group (USA) Inc.
375 Hudson Street, New York, New York 10014, USA
Penguin Group (Canada), 90 Eglinton Avenue East, Suite 700, Toronto, Ontario M4P 2Y3, Canada
(a division of Pearson Penguin Canada Inc.)
Penguin Books Ltd., 80 Strand, London WC2R 0RL, England
Penguin Group Ireland, 25 St. Stephen's Green, Dublin 2, Ireland (a division of Penguin Books Ltd.)
Penguin Group (Australia), 250 Camberwell Road, Camberwell, Victoria 3124, Australia
(a division of Pearson Australia Group Pty. Ltd.)
Penguin Books India Pvt. Ltd., 11 Community Centre, Panchsheel Park, New Delhi—110 017, India
Penguin Group (NZ), Cnr. Airborne and Rosedale Roads, Albany, Auckland 1310, New Zealand
(a division of Pearson New Zealand Ltd.)
Penguin Books (South Africa) (Pty.) Ltd., 24 Sturdee Avenue, Rosebank, Johannesburg 2196,
South Africa

Penguin Books Ltd., Registered Offices: 80 Strand, London WC2R 0RL, England

This is a work of fiction. Names, characters, places, and incidents either are the product of the author's imagination or are used fictitiously, and any resemblance to actual persons, living or dead, business establishments, events, or locales is entirely coincidental.

ALIVE OR NOTHING

A Jove Book / published by arrangement with the author

PRINTING HISTORY
Jove edition / April 2006

ISBN: 0-515-14123-2

JOVE®
Jove Books are published by The Berkley Publishing Group,
a division of Penguin Group (USA) Inc.,
375 Hudson Street, New York, New York 10014.
JOVE is a registered trademark of Penguin Group (USA) Inc.
The "J" design is a trademark belonging to Penguin Group (USA) Inc.

PRINTED IN THE UNITED STATES OF AMERICA

10 9 8 7 6 5 4 3 2 1

ONE

"Where's my money?"

The question came from the shadows, as if the darkness itself was trying to squeeze ten thousand dollars from John Grinbee. When he heard the question, Grinbee's first instinct was to lie. Unfortunately, he knew better than to try such a foolish stunt against a man like Zack Richards.

"I don't have it with me," Grinbee said. "At least, not all of it."

The silence that followed played hell on Grinbee's ears. It surrounded the portly man like a glove that gripped him tighter and tighter with each second that passed. Finally, the grip eased up enough for Grinbee to pull in another breath.

"That's not what I wanted to hear," came the voice from the shadows. Suddenly, those shadows moved as a man stepped forward to allow his face to be seen. "You should know better than to disappoint me, Senator."

Hearing his title uttered aloud caused Grinbee to cast nervous glances in all directions. The only other people he saw within earshot were the menacing gun hands who'd cut Grinbee off from the rest of the world.

Looking around at those grim faces, Grinbee found himself laughing under his breath. It was a nervous, trembling laughter that could barely be heard over the rustling night breeze.

At that moment, Grinbee felt more like he was in an animal's den than the backroom of a cathouse. All around him, the noises of a happier world could be heard. There was a banjo playing, women laughing and men spouting steam to try and impress them. The door to the backroom wasn't even closed, allowing Grinbee to spot the occasional working girl leading her next customer to the bedrooms down the hall.

The backroom was all business, however. There was nothing on the walls and only one bookshelf stocked with dozens of identical ledgers. There was no desk and only a pair of uncomfortable chairs along one wall. The only source of light was a candle on top of a small circular table by the door, which left most of the room to Grinbee's imagination.

Now that he'd stepped forward, Zack Richards could barely be distinguished from the shadows. His face was narrow and his eyes were intense slits. His hawk-like nose protruded over a dark mustache which ran all the way down both sides of his mouth to his chin.

"I'd . . . prefer if you didn't call me that," Grinbee said.

When Zack smiled, it caused his lip to curl slightly and reveal a set of thin, pointed teeth. "Call you what? 'Senator'? Didn't you work hard to get that title?"

"Yes, but . . . never mind."

Zack nodded and kept his grin in place. "I get it. You don't want anyone to know you're here."

"Of course I don't," Grinbee snapped. "And you know that damn well enough."

"I sure do know it. That's why it's unfortunate that you chose to stiff me tonight. If things don't go right, a whole lot of people will know you're here. They'll also know all about your dealings with me and how you arranged for the death of Dan Gray."

Grinbee winced at the sound of that name. "Dan Gray? What's he got to do with any of this?"

"From what I hear, he's the one man in your jurisdiction who's got a prayer of knocking you out of office once the next elections roll around."

"Possibly. So what?"

Taking another step forward, Zack didn't even bother trying to hide how much he was enjoying himself. "So, that's why folks won't have any trouble believing that you had poor Dan Gray shot down in cold blood."

"I would never!"

"Maybe not," Zack said with a shrug. "But that's just between you and me. Who knows? Maybe nobody will believe it. Maybe folks just love you so much that they won't tolerate hearing one word spoken against you." Zack's shoulders twitched as he let out a grunting laugh. "Or maybe your days of being a politician will be over. I can't think of many men that could bounce back from a smudge like that on their record. But maybe I'm wrong in your case."

As he listened to Zack's words, Grinbee started to sweat. His career had had its shared of ups and downs, but had been fairly stable over the last ten years. Like any politician worth his salt, he'd acquired more than a few enemies along the way, and if one of them showed up dead, it wouldn't look too good.

"You're bluffing," Grinbee said.

"You want to try me?"

Grinbee shook his head before uttering another word. "No, but this is all unnecessary. I can get your money. I just don't have it all with me at the moment."

"Where is it?"

"Here," Grinbee said as he reached into his jacket pocket.

The moment Grinbee's hand slipped into his jacket, the other men in the room reached for their weapons, and quickly had a finger on their triggers.

Zack nodded to the other men and reached out to slap away Grinbee's hand. From there, he pulled open Grinbee's jacket and found the bundle the senator had been after. Once he took the bundle, Zack shoved Grinbee aside.

"What's in here?" Zack asked.

"Ten thousand dollars," Grinbee quickly replied. "I can get the rest for you in a week or so."

Zack's eyes were fixed on Grinbee. When they narrowed a bit more, it was similar to sunlight being focused through a magnifying glass.

"F-five days!" Grinbee spat. "I can get the rest in five days. It'll be rough, but I should be able to pull it off."

"Five days?" Zack took a moment to ponder that notion. Finally, he nodded and said, "All right. If you can get it for me in five days, then that should cover it."

"Really? Then we're all squared up?"

"Sure. Thirty thousand in five days should do it just fine."

Although Grinbee looked happy for a few moments, his cheer started to dissipate within another few seconds. "Don't you mean twenty-five thousand in five days? I mean, considering the payment you have right there?"

Zack shook his head. "This money here is enough to buy you some more time. I expect you to pay me a full thirty thousand in five days. Otherwise, we might just have to come to another arrangement."

Grinbee let out a breath that left him slouching and clenching his eyes shut. "What kind of arrangement?"

"Let's just say you could skip out of here and forget about scrounging up any more money. In return, you can do me the occasional favor when I need a service that only a senator can provide."

"What kind of service?"

When Zack stepped forward, he moved as quickly as a snake striking from tall grass. "Whatever damn service I ask you to do. Otherwise, everyone from the president to the drunks in your hometown will know about your dirty past. Before that dust settles, you'll have a whole other heap of shit dumped on your shoulders that you'll never be able to dig out of. So don't fucking question me again or I'll just have one of my boys shoot a hole through your head right now and be done with it. Understand?"

"Y-yes. I understand."

"Good. I'll see you in five days. You'll either have some money for me or an agreement for our other arrangement."

Although he'd never actually had a noose around his neck, Grinbee was getting a real good idea of how it felt to be in such a position.

TWO

"I can't breathe in this," Clint said as he dug a finger underneath the bow tie that had been wrapped around his neck.

"Here," said a woman wearing a purple velvet dress as she reached out to fix Clint's tie. "Let me get that for you."

Standing up straight, Clint let the woman do her work as he took advantage of his wonderful view. Karen Vatterov had the dark, flowing hair of a gypsy, and a body that could have made a burlap sack look like the latest Paris fashion.

Her full, red lips were curled into a smile as she fussed with the tie around Clint's neck. Her chestnut hair flowed back over one shoulder and spilled across the front of the other. A silk rose was pinned over one ear to keep one section of her wavy hair in place.

"There," she said. "How's that?"

Clint rolled his head a bit, but wasn't able to ditch the feeling that he was being slowly strangled. "It's a little better, but not great."

Giving the bow tie one more adjustment, Karen brushed Clint's shoulders and said, "You look fine and that's all that matters. You can be comfortable after the ball."

Clint reached out to place both hands upon her hips. Although she squirmed a bit, the motion of her body gave no indication that she was actually trying to get away from him. "Are you sure we can't get out of this thing?" he asked. "I'm not too big on formal events."

Karen's hands moved down Clint's shoulders and over his arms. She slipped her hands back up until she was able to slide her fingers through his hair. "This isn't just some dinner party. It's a ball being thrown by the governor of Colorado and we are going."

"Did it have to be thrown in summer? I'm already sweating in this damn getup."

"For your information," she said while easing her hands along Clint's chest, "you look absolutely wonderful in that suit. Besides, you wear thicker clothes when you ride up into the mountains. What's the matter? You're only comfortable when you smell like a horse?"

"Hey! There's nothing wrong with the way Eclipse smells."

Karen rolled her eyes. "Is that so?"

Clint smirked and leaned down until his face was brushing against the nape of Karen's neck. "Then again, there are a few other things that smell a whole lot better."

Her skin smelled like lilacs, which was the perfume she'd bought less than a week ago. As Clint slowly moved his lips along the line of her neck, he could feel her leaning back against his arms and her hair tickling his cheek.

Karen let out a soft moan when she felt Clint's arms wrap around her and his lips brush against the skin of her exposed shoulder. "Are you trying to distract me?"

Allowing his eyes to follow the plunging neckline of her dress, Clint slid his hands up until he was cupping one of her large breasts. "Maybe."

"Mmm. Then you're doing a good job," Karen said as she pressed her hips against Clint's body. With just a few slow grinds, she could feel his penis becoming erect through his dark dress pants. Soon, she was reaching down to stroke him until he was stiff as a board.

"And if you want to spend the night with me," she whispered, "you'll have to go to the Governor's Ball and act like you're having a good time."

Clint pressed his eyes shut and let out a measured breath. "You are an evil woman."

Karen smiled and once again straightened Clint's tie, using both hands. In the next moment, she was standing up straight and taking a few steps back so she could get a better look at him. "And you are a very handsome man. Are you going to accompany me to the Governor's Ball?"

Now that the blood was flowing through his brain again, Clint nodded. "I guess I might as well, since I'm already strapped into this suit."

Karen was already turning around and heading back to the little vanity on the other side of the room. "That's what I like to hear."

The room was the biggest in the Denver Grand Hotel. On one side was the biggest bed Clint had seen in a few years. On the other were a few little tables and bureaus. The vanity at which Karen was standing had a tall, oval mirror in a walnut frame. As she looked into the glass, she made sure every strand of hair was in place and that her lips were just the right shade of red.

"This may be considered blackmail," Clint said as he stepped close enough to get a look at himself in one of the smaller mirrors on the wall. "After all, you never mentioned a thing about any of this when you asked me to visit you."

Karen's reflection smiled at Clint. "Would you have really refused if I had mentioned it?"

"Maybe."

She laughed and got back to fussing with her hair. "If it makes you feel any better, I didn't know about it until just before you arrived."

"I've been in Denver for three days," Clint said as he moved up behind her and slipped his hands around her waist. "The first I heard about the ball was this morning."

"Guess it must have slipped my mind. We have been pretty busy, after all."

"Yes we have." Clint's hands ran up and down along her hips before sliding over her stomach and up to the generous curves of her breasts. "Speaking of that, when do we have to leave for the ball?"

"In about half an hour," Karen said. "But don't get any ideas. I've still got to get ready."

"You look fine," Clint whispered into her ear.

"It's not every day I get invited to things like this, Clint. I need to make sure everything is just right and if I'm going to do that, I can't look away from this mirror."

Both of Clint's hands moved down and disappeared from Karen's sight. "Who said a thing about you leaving this spot?" Clint asked as he slowly eased Karen's skirts up over her hips.

THREE

Karen's skirts made a soft rustle as Clint moved them up to reveal the smooth curves underneath the layers of silk and velvet. Her legs were shapely and covered in stockings that were the same color as the flower in her hair. Moving the skirts up a little more revealed the little silk strands of her garter, which pointed the way up toward her waist.

"Clint Adams, what do you think you're doing?" Although her words were meant to be stern, the voice in which they were spoken sounded more like a purr.

Clint smiled as he eased her skirts up higher. His eyes drank in the sight of her plump backside which was barely covered by another layer of thin silk. The garter curved around the sides of her buttocks and went all the way up to a lacy belt which framed her assets perfectly.

"If you don't know what I'm doing," Clint said, "then you haven't been paying attention for the last few days."

"Clint, I need to do this to get ready."

"Then just tell me to stop and I will."

Although he could hear Karen pulling in a breath as he slid his hand along the inside of her thigh, he didn't hear her say one word to make him stop what he was doing. In fact, as she felt him move his hand up higher, Karen bent forward and moved her legs apart.

Clint could feel her skin getting warmer the higher he went. Once his fingers brushed against the downy hair between her legs, he also felt the smooth lips of her pussy getting wetter. With his free hand, he unbuckled his pants and lowered them.

Turning to look at him over her shoulder, Karen tossed her hair back and fixed her brown eyes upon him. In the mirror, Clint got a breathtaking view of her cleavage as she arched her back and grabbed hold of the sides of the vanity.

With one hand, Clint rubbed her vagina until she was slick and ready for him. With his other hand, he guided the tip of his cock between her legs until he just started to enter her.

Karen bit down on her lower lip and moved her legs apart a little more. She didn't take her eyes off of him as she felt every inch of his rigid penis slide into her. She gripped the vanity even harder and let out a slow, breathy moan.

Now that he was all the way inside of her, Clint settled his hands upon Karen's hips and grabbed hold. As he started moving in and out of her, he pulled her hips so that she bumped against him when he thrust forward. Her backside was perfectly shaped and just wide enough to give her body an hourglass shape. Before too long, Karen reached back to take hold of her skirts so they would stay out of Clint's way as he tended to more important matters.

The suite was lit by several lanterns nailed to the walls, bathing the large room in a soothing, golden light. A few shadows flickered over Karen's back, but the flames made her skin look lightly tanned in comparison to the folds of material bunched up around her waist.

Clint moved one hand onto the small of her back as he started pumping into her a little harder. When Karen tossed her hair and lifted her head to let out another satisfied groan, Clint took hold of her hair and pulled, just the way he knew she liked it.

Sure enough, Karen smiled at the mirror as she grunted every time Clint pounded into her. She opened her eyes to study her own body and face before noticing that Clint had his eyes closed in concentration.

Karen's body was hot and soft to the touch. It was a combination that made it difficult for Clint to keep his distance from her. Luckily, he hadn't needed to worry about doing any such thing since he'd arrived. Not only was she a pleasure to the touch, but she knew him just as well as he knew her.

Once she saw Clint open his eyes, Karen straightened up a little and peeled the front of her dress down to expose her large, rounded breasts. She smiled when she saw the hungry look in Clint's eyes and then moved her hands along the sides of her breasts as he continued to pump into her from behind. With the tips of her fingers, she teased her nipples until they were fully erect.

Letting out a groan of his own, Clint eased out of her and pulled her away from the vanity so he could turn her around. Karen's hair twirled around her, landing onto her shoulders in a wild cascade of soft waves.

"You're in trouble now," Karen said, even as she adjusted herself so that she was sitting on the edge of the vanity.

"Trust me, you look amazing."

A mischievous smile slipped onto Karen's face as she spread her legs open wide for Clint. "Really?"

"Yes," Clint said as he settled between her legs and ran his hands along her hips. "Really."

As Clint leaned forward to kiss her passionately on the mouth, he felt Karen's hand encircle his cock and guide it back into her. Rather than slide it all the way into her right away, Clint teased her by pushing in just a little and then easing back out again. He did that until he felt her start to squirm. The insistent motions of Karen's lower body practically begged for him to give her what she wanted.

Unable to hold out much longer himself, Clint grabbed hold of her hips and pumped into her with enough force to rattle the vanity as well as everything on top of it. Karen wrapped her legs around him and leaned back as far as she could, while pulling her skirts up over her waist. Soon, she began pumping her hips in time to Clint's rhythm as she let out a moan that filled the entire suite.

Before too long, her breath started coming in short, gasping bursts. Her eyes clenched shut and sweat trickled down the front of her body. Karen's body shuddered as she climaxed and let out a breath that she'd been holding for a few seconds.

Clint could feel her clench around him. A few more thrusts was all it took for him to feel that same pleasure course through him. Grabbing onto her hips and pounding forward once more, he exploded inside of her. When he opened his eyes, he saw Karen looking back at him with a wild, enthusiastic smile on her face.

"We'd better get going," Clint said, exhausting every bit of self-control he could muster. "Or else we're going to be late."

FOUR

The Governor's Ball was held at a large mansion in the
older section of town. Although it wasn't an official gov-
ernmental affair, there were enough politicians in atten-
dance to start another war. Clint and Karen stopped just
short of entering the ballroom so they could take in all the
sights and sounds filling the high-ceilinged space.

"This is fancy," Karen said under her breath. "Even
more than I was expecting."

"Excuse me, sir," came a voice from Clint's left.

When he turned to get a look at who'd spoken, Clint
saw a man with a square jaw casting a stern glare in his direction. "Can I help you?" Clint asked.

"Yes, sir. You can hand over your firearm."

Clint's hand drifted to the holster at his side. Having the
modified Colt at his hip was more than just second nature
to him. The pistol was as much a part of him as the hand
that carried it. Being asked to give it up didn't set too well
with him. Considering the event, Clint got over his reaction pretty quickly and did something he very rarely did.

"Sorry about that," he said, while unbuckling the holster. "Take good care of it."

The square-jawed man glanced at the pistol and narrowed his eyes. "Looks like you've made some changes to that model."

"You noticed?"

"I've seen a hundred Colts and have stripped down every last one of them. I've wanted to speed up the action on the hammer, but never quite knew my way around it. Looks like a fairly good job."

Clint shrugged and said, "Some of the newer models can match the performance I gave that one."

"Sure, but no stock model gun can compare to something that's been crafted by a man who knows what he's doing."

Karen cleared her throat. "If you two would like to be alone, I'll just step inside and find someone else to take me to the dance floor."

Clint rolled his eyes just enough for the guard at the door to catch his meaning. Although the square-jawed man maintained his stern expression, he looked awfully close to allowing a smirk onto his face.

Wrapping her arm tightly around Clint's, Karen pulled him into the ballroom a few steps before stopping once again. Once inside, the sights and sounds enveloped them. There was a string quartet playing in an alcove to one side, dozens of conversations taking place, and laughter mixed throughout. The men seemed to have been poured from the same mold and painted the same shade of black. The women, on the other hand, represented nearly every color of the rainbow and were gussied up even more by sparkling jewels and sequins.

"Have you seen anything like this?" Karen asked under her breath.

Clint tugged at his tie to get some air. "Not for a while. It's been campfires and baked beans for me for a long time. Tell you the truth, I can't rightly say that's looking so bad right about now."

"Oh, stop fussing. Come on! I see the governor talking to Senator Gray."

"Looks like this place is filled with important people," Clint said.

"Really? Do you recognize a lot of them?"

"Not a lot, but it's easy enough to spot the best-dressed fellows surrounded by boot-lickers."

As Karen pulled him through the crowd, Clint managed to snag some kind of pastry off a tray to go with the glass of champagne he was handed. When they reached the men Karen had spotted, she was smiling brightly enough to light the room. The men started off with grins on their faces, but didn't seem quite so happy to see Clint.

"Hello, Governor," she said with a curtsy. "Lovely party."

The governor didn't strike Clint as much different from the other politicians there. He was in his late fifties or early sixties with a head of silver, well tended hair. His mustache was perfectly trimmed and he had an air of superiority hanging over his head like a smoke cloud.

"Hello, there, Karen. Who's this with you?"

"This is Clint Adams."

Clint offered his hand. Surprisingly enough, the governor accepted it quickly.

"Clint Adams?" the governor asked. "Are you 'the Gunsmith'?"

"Some call me that, yes. Although, I wouldn't believe everything you read about me."

"From what I hear, you're quite an impressive fellow."

"Well, then," Clint said, "believe it all."

Both of them laughed, but the governor kept it going a bit longer. When he managed to compose himself, the governor nodded toward the other man standing at his side. "Clint Adams, this is Senator Dan Gray. He's a good friend of mine."

Clint shook the senator's hand. "Honored."

"Likewise," Gray said. "I've heard a few things about

you, myself from some acquaintances with the Secret Service."

"I've done a few jobs with them," Clint replied. "Not that I had any choice, of course."

That got another round of laughs from the politicians. When it was over, Senator Gray looked away from the rest and stopped laughing.

"As much as I hate to," Gray said, "I'm afraid I need to excuse myself. Pleased to meet you, Mister Adams." He took Karen's hand and kissed it politely. "You too, ma'am."

The moment Gray let her hand go, Karen felt another close around it.

"I'd be honored if I could have this dance," the governor said.

Karen looked over to Clint with pleading eyes. He responded to the silent question with a friendly nod. "Go on," he said. "I'm going to try and scrounge up something to eat."

As the governor escorted her to the dance floor, Karen smiled and batted her eyelashes at the older man. When his arms encircled her, the governor pulled her close and started a slow twirl about the room. Karen was already whispering in his ear when Clint spotted a long table holding an appetizing spread of meats and cheeses.

FIVE

An hour later, the ball was still going at full swing. The men still stood about in their dark suits, while the ladies showed off their finery on or around the dance floor. There were a few exceptions to this rule, including the people serving the food and drinks as well as the men standing guard at the doors.

Clint was another of these exceptions. After gaining favor with the guards by bringing them a plate of food, he found that he had much more in common with those men than with the politicians inside the ball.

The square-jawed man at the front door was named John. Once everyone had arrived at the ball, he had little else to do besides stand around with his arms crossed. When Clint had arrived with the food, more guards had shown up. One of the men had dug a deck of cards from his pocket, which had made the night take a turn for the better.

"I hope none of you will get in trouble for this," Clint said as he took a sip of wine and tossed away two of his five cards.

John shook his head and tossed one of his own cards. "All the doors are still covered. Hell, being all clumped together like this, we're guarding the front entrance better than before."

"Good point."

"What brings you over here, Clint? I mean, you don't seem like the sort who gets all giddy when he sees some old geezer from Washington."

"I'm a friend of Karen Vatterov."

John's brow furrowed as he fit in the replacement cards he was dealt. "Why does that name sound familiar?"

"She runs Vatterov's Varieties a few blocks from here."

"Oh yeah! That's a hell of a nice place. The girls there really know what they're doing."

One of the other guards sitting at the game chuckled under his breath. "They also know how to wring a good living from most of the politicians in there."

"I wouldn't know anything about that," Clint said. Although it was something of a lie, he didn't bother keeping track of every deal Karen had made in her life. He did know that she'd come to some sort of arrangement to stay in business as well as draw in twice as much money as she claimed to earn.

John was laughing too. "Well, it's hard for us to not know about that sort of thing. We spend just as much time guarding those idiots from their wives as we do from any assassins or the like. Most of the fellas I look after get their girls delivered to them."

"Not me," the youngest guard said. "I spend so much time at Vatterov's that I get free drinks."

All five of the men huddled over their cards laughed at that one. After a few more rounds of betting, Clint wound up taking the pot, which consisted of a dollar and twenty-eight cents. The cards were dealt and a bald man with a beak-like nose offered everyone cigars.

Clint refused the cigar at first, but got it shoved right back at him.

"I used to serve down at Fort Laramie," the bald guard said. "Some of my buddies told me about how you helped them out down there a while ago."

It took a moment, but the details came right back into Clint's mind. "Oh yeah. Fort Laramie. Those were some fine soldiers. A few were lost in that business, but it got straightened out."

"You're damn right it did and you did plenty of the straightening. You'll smoke that cigar with me and take my thanks."

Although none of the other guards knew the faces and names that the bald man referred to, they were all ex-soldiers and nodded solemnly in Clint's direction. Clint took the cigar and was almost knocked off the little crate he used as a stool by a hearty pat on the back from the guard who lit his cigar.

"So, Miss Vatterov dragged you out here, huh?" John asked.

Fanning his cards in front of him, Clint said, "I was in the area and we go back a long way."

"But you don't look too comfortable in that suit."

"This isn't my first choice, but she does have a way of convincing folks."

"Convincing men, you mean," the bald guard said.

"Yeah." Clint chuckled. "You can say that. Anyway, this is more of a business night for her. She needed a word with the governor."

The guards nodded.

Breathing out a stream of bitter smoke, John said, "Them politicians got their way of doing things and it sure as hell ain't the way they promised when they got elected. I can't say they're all crooked, but they're a far cry from being straight arrows."

"That's how I figure it," Clint said. "I know Karen isn't the sort to step too far out of line. But if some judge or politician steps out on his wife or gets caught doing the wrong thing in the wrong place, perhaps he deserves to pay for it one way or another."

"And your friend Miss Vatterov gets to take in the profits?" the youngest guard asked.

"Better her than someone who'd make an even bigger mess out of things," Clint replied. "I'm not going to lend a hand in any of that mess, but it wasn't her that started it. Besides, all Karen's getting out of this is a few silent partners in her establishment. If she was into anything too bad, she'd be pulling in a whole lot more money than that."

"Eh, to hell with 'em," the bald guard grunted as he folded his hand. "There ain't no way to deal with a politician without getting your hands dirty. I know for a fact that Miss Vatterov keeps the governor and plenty of others too busy to stir up too much shit. More power to her."

"It ain't a perfect system, but it's all we got," John said. "So long as the important matters get handled, I'll keep them geezers safe."

The youngest of the group shook his head and looked over to a guard whose face was covered with dark brown whiskers. The rest of the burly man's head was covered by a gray, wide-brimmed hat.

"What about you, Ed?" the young guard asked. "You ain't even said a word through all of this."

Ed looked around at each man in turn before shifting his eyes right back to his cards. "Politicians are gonna screw the taxpayers along with anything in a skirt. Ain't nothing new."

Clint tipped his hat to the surly man behind the beard. "Now those are some true words of wisdom."

"Senator Gray's a good man," the youngest guard said. "I've never seen him step out on his wife or meet with any shady types."

"Then he's got nothing to worry about," John said. "A man in a hole don't get there unless he steps in it himself.

Now let's get back to the game. If I wanted to talk politics, I'd be inside with the rest of them windbags."

Although the group started laughing at that, all of them quieted up in a heartbeat. Clint was a little behind the rest, but he felt the nervous tension ripple through the men like an invisible wave. When he looked around, he saw that all the guards were getting to their feet.

"No need to salute," Senator Gray said jokingly. "I'm just out for a breath of fresh air. You men enjoying the ball?"

"Yes, sir," the young guard replied as he fell into step with the senator.

"Good." With that, along with a friendly wave, Senator Gray moved along.

All the guards slowly lowered themselves back onto their seats. All of them except for John. His square jaw clenched tightly as he watched the senator and his guard move down the path that led back to the street.

"Come on back," said one of the guards who'd kept quiet until now. "It'll be a while before this thing's over." Wire-rimmed spectacles sat atop a thick nose on his solid face. He was built more like a mule than a man, and held his cards as if they were scraps stuck to his fingers.

"Somethin' ain't right," John said.

Clint got to his feet and looked in the direction John was facing. He couldn't see anyone in the shadows or on the path. Even Senator Gray and his guard had moved out of sight. "What is it?" Clint asked.

John's face crunched up a bit as he replied, "Can't rightly say. Just a feeling, I guess."

"I got a feeling too," Ed grunted. "I got a feeling I'm about to win you boys' money."

"Deal me out," Clint said.

"Stay here, Adams," John ordered. "This isn't your job."

"You owe me a buck fifty," Clint replied. "I need to protect my investment."

"Sit back down and play your hand," John insisted. "My job's to keep the folks here safe, and that includes you."

"Looks like it may be a little late for that," Clint said.

John started to say something, but stopped short when he heard rustling coming from almost every direction. As he shifted around on the balls of his feet, he saw dark figures emerge from either side of the path that led down to the street. Moonlight glinted off the bared iron in the men's hands.

SIX

"You men stay put and no one will get hurt," came a voice from one of the dark figures.

Now that they'd made their appearance, the figures could be seen as something more than just shadows. There were four of them in all. Each man wore dark clothes with a mask to cover his face and his hat pulled down low to conceal it further. Two men carried pistols, while the other two had rifles.

Ed straightened up to his full height. That alone made him look more like a bear than a man. "Step aside and let me pass," Ed growled.

"You'll stay put," came the same voice as before.

Even now, Clint couldn't tell exactly which of the four men were speaking.

John's eyes snapped from the men in front of him to the path that stretched out into the darkness. After less than a second had passed, he clenched his fists and rushed forward.

The other men were clearly surprised by the sudden charge and two of them even took a reflexive step aside. The remaining two planted their feet and reacted to John's attack. One of them managed to pull the trigger of their pistol, but the other was too busy getting knocked onto his ass.

As that single shot thundered into the night, all hell was unleashed. Ed dropped his hand to the pistol at his side while also lowering himself to one knee. One of the masked men took a shot at him, but hadn't adjusted his aim to Ed's new position and the shot went over the guard's head.

Two of the other masked men fired their weapons. One of those shots found its mark in the guard who'd been the quietest of the bunch. Clint didn't even know the name of the man who was knocked backward off his stool to land in a heap on the ground. After kicking a few times and grabbing at the bloody wound in his chest, the guard let out a final breath and gazed up at the sky.

Clint acted on sheer instinct. Since he didn't have his Colt, he ducked low and prayed to survive through the first round of gunfire. Hot lead screamed over and around him. The blood rushed through Clint's ears, but he managed to set that aside as he worked his way toward the closest masked figure.

A body slammed against the ground, but not because of catching a bullet. John was kneeling beside the fallen masked man and was already sending a beefy fist down into the man's face. Gritting his teeth as the man beneath him smashed the handle of his gun into his ribs, John lashed out with another punch. This time, his knuckles practically lodged themselves into the masked man's skull, bouncing it against the ground.

One of the masked men close to John turned to shift his aim in that guard's direction. His arm was stopped short, however, when Clint grabbed it by the wrist and forced it upward. The gun went off once, illuminating the determined glare etched across Clint's features.

Keeping hold of the masked man's wrist, Clint sent one

of his knees straight up into the guy's stomach. Although he heard a pained grunt from behind the mask, Clint felt like he'd just kicked a tree stump. Pain spiked through his leg, and Clint felt himself being pulled off his feet as the man in front of him tried to reclaim his arm.

"Hold on, Adams!" Ed shouted as he worked his way to where Clint was struggling. "I'm almost there."

Clint felt the arm he was dangling from start to swing in Ed's direction. As much as he tried to stop it, Clint knew he wouldn't be able to do anything of the sort with just the grip he had around the man's wrist.

The man with whom Clint had chosen to tangle wasn't much taller than he was, but he seemed to have been built from nothing less than bricks and mortar. No matter how much Clint tried to divert the man's gun hand or shove the guy off balance, he couldn't seem to uproot the attacker.

Finally, Clint stopped trying to chop down the mountain and took a different approach. The seconds had been dragging by and he was afraid he was out of time before that trigger was pulled. Clint didn't have to be looking down the barrel of the other man's gun to know that Ed was about to get himself shot at any moment.

Clint reached up with both hands to take hold of the pistol in the masked man's grasp. Then, with one brutal twist, he wrenched the gun around in a way that the man's hand wasn't meant to bend. He felt something snap and heard a wet crunch as the gunman let out a pained scream.

The gun went off, but its barrel was already pointed at the ground. Ed stomped forward, completely ignoring the dirt that got kicked up less than a few inches from his boots.

"Out of the way, goddammit," Ed snarled as he shoved Clint aside.

Not only was Clint happy to oblige, but he was eager to see what was happening with the other men.

John fired another shot, which caught another of the

masked men in the shoulder. Before that one could respond with the rifle he carried, John sent another shot in his direction, which dropped the man straight to the ground. When he caught sight of Clint, he raised his pistol and hollered, "Get down!"

Clint dropped reflexively as two shots blazed over his head. One of those shots came from John, but the other came from the shadows behind Clint's position. Even as he was headed toward the ground, Clint could see that there were more problems than the original bunch that had stepped out of the darkness.

There were at least two others emerging from a different spot and they were already firing at the remaining guards. Clint rolled toward one of the men who'd fallen and snatched up the rifle that was no longer in use. Sighting over the body of the masked man who'd brought the rifle in the first place, Clint took aim and fired.

One of the two masked men in the distance was knocked down like a bottle from atop a fence post.

"Here," John said as he walked by. "Take this. We're going to check on Senator Gray."

Although the gun he was given wasn't his own Colt, Clint accepted the weapon and quickly tucked it into his inner jacket pocket. "Not without me, you're not."

Neither of the remaining guards were inclined to argue.

SEVEN

The path that led to the street was lined on both sides by tall trees. In the dark, however, those trees might as well have been walls put up specifically to keep anyone from seeing what was going on off the path. All three of the men slowed their steps and kept quiet so they could hear the first sign of movement. With their ears still ringing from the recent gunfire, however, that was much easier said than done.

John was at the front of the group, and when he stopped, the other two quickly followed suit. Clint was right behind him and Ed was at the rear. When John held up his hand and pointed to the left of the path, Ed nodded and moved off in that direction.

Clint patted John on the shoulder and nodded toward a spot farther up the trail. The shadows were especially thick in that area, but the sounds of voices and footsteps could be heard from that direction. Crouching low and spreading out a bit, John and Clint worked their way toward those voices as quickly as they could without making too much noise of their own.

After too many steps were taken, Clint could start to make out words from the hurried rush of whispered sounds coming from ahead.

". . . don't have to do this. I can pay whatever you—"

"Shut up. Don't need . . . damn word."

Clint guessed the first one to speak was Senator Gray. He couldn't make a guess about the second one.

Now that they were getting closer, the voices were getting easier to understand. In fact, Clint could just make out the shapes of two figures standing in a clearing just past the first row of trees. One of them was standing facing the path while the other was on his knees.

"Please. Just let him go." This one was Senator Gray. Clint was certain of it now.

"I said shut up," the unidentified man snarled in a fierce whisper. Rather than say another word, the figure raised his outstretched arm. The next sound to drift through the air was the metallic click of a pistol's hammer being thumbed back.

In front of Clint, John crouched a bit lower and brought his own gun up. With his free hand, he motioned for Clint to move around to the right. John didn't wait to see if his order had been seen or would be followed before he rushed toward the clearing.

Clint was in motion before John was even done pointing and picked out his path as his feet hurried along it.

"What the hell?" the gunman next to Senator Gray grunted as he spotted something busting out of the trees.

Being the stoutest man of all the guards, Ed didn't even bother trying to conceal his approach. He simply rushed forward when he got as close as he could get. He exploded from the trees like an angry bear, firing off a shot as he moved.

Ed's shot was high, but it served its purpose well enough. As hot lead whipped through the air over his head, the man holding the gun on Senator Gray ducked down and to the side, while shifting his aim away from the kneeling politician.

At this time, John stepped out of the trees and took a

shot of his own. The gunman still had his eyes focused on
Ed, so the sight of John coming at him from a different angle put a look of panic on the man's face. That panic was
matched only by Senator Gray, who was looking around as
if the sky was falling in large chunks all around him.

"Don't kill me!" Senator Gray screamed as he wrapped
his arms over his head and hunkered down into a ball.
"Please don't shoot me!"

As soon as he got within arm's reach of the senator,
John placed one hand on the politician's shoulders and
shoved him down until Gray was laying flat on his belly.
John kept his palm on the senator's back as he took aim
and fired once more at the gunman.

By this time, Ed had charged far enough to lower his
head like a bull and slam his shoulder into the gunman's
stomach. The man squeezed off another shot, but was too
confused to hit anything besides one of the many trees surrounding him.

Watching all of this as though he wasn't even a part of
it, John held his position, even as shots were fired all
around him. His eyes snapped a little to his left as he spotted something moving in the shadows. When he saw an unfamiliar face, as well as the glint of a gun barrel, John
aimed and fired. That face was knocked back into the darkness, followed by the sound of something heavy hitting the
dirt.

Taking hold of the gunman in one hand, Ed brought the
butt of his pistol down to crack against the other man's
wrist. The gunman's pistol hit the ground and was immediately covered by Ed's boot. Now that he was unarmed, the
gunman wasn't able to hide the fear in his eyes as he was
lifted off his feet.

"Where's the kid?" Ed asked.

The gunman did his best to suck in a breath or two, but
was only able to get a few gulps of air. "Wh-what kid?"

"Don't play stupid with me!" Ed snarled as he shook

the gunman like a rag doll. "The kid that was with the senator. The kid guarding Senator Gray!"

Although the gunman managed to keep quiet, he couldn't prevent his eyes from darting over to the ground nearby.

When Ed got a look for himself, he gritted his teeth and tightened his grip on the gunman.

"I know, Ed," John said in a level voice. "I saw him too. We need to tend to our duties before we worry about—"

Just then, another shot cracked through the air. But this one didn't come from any of the men in the clearing. Instead, it came from the trees and sent a spray of leaves in every direction as a bullet chewed through the surrounding greenery.

Before anyone could react to that, something else came flying into the clearing. This was no bullet, however, but a body. The man was skinny and flailing like a bird with its feathers plucked as he was launched headfirst from where he'd been hiding.

"That's the only one I could find," Clint said as he stepped out from the same spot the skinny man had come from. "But my guess is there's probably more lurking around."

John grinned and nodded his approval. That smirk disappeared real quickly when he shifted his gaze to the first gunman. "How many more are there?"

The gunman didn't give John anything more than a sneer. That changed real quickly once Ed reminded him about the position he was in.

"You heard the question, asshole," Ed growled. "You'd best answer it!"

"Just one more," the gunman replied. "But he's long gone by now."

John's eyes shifted toward Clint. "Would you mind, Adams? We've got our hands full here just now."

Clint was already searching the shadows as much as he

could from where he stood. Now that the shooting had
stopped, he could hear plenty of sounds coming from the
surrounding area. Unfortunately, most of those sounds
were alarmed voices coming from the nearby mansion.

"Clint? You hear me?" John asked.

Although Clint nodded a bit, he didn't take his eyes
from a break in the trees no more than six paces from
where Ed was hoisting the gunman. When he'd first spotted that dark shape, Clint thought it was another tree or
maybe an animal. But now that his eyes were adjusted to
the night, he could make out a few more details to convince
him otherwise.

When Clint took a step toward the shadow, that dark
form turned and bolted in the opposite direction. Clint tore
straight after it.

EIGHT

Clint had spent enough time in camps to know how tricky shadows could be. Sometimes a rock formation could look like a herd of buffalo or a fallen log could resemble a stack of dead bodies. Plenty of ghost stories got started by things like that and plenty of tree stumps had been shot when a tired hunter mistook them for a deer.

But one thing Clint knew for certain was that no deer wore a bowler hat and cursed under its breath as it stumbled while trying to get away.

Having spotted the bowler hat moments before the shadow turned and ran, Clint bolted after it to hear those curses coming from whoever was trying to make his escape.

The ground was lumpy and thick with tangled roots that grabbed at Clint's feet as he ran. After a few near-spills of his own, Clint took his finger off the trigger and concentrated on catching up to the shadowy form in front of him.

Whoever it was either had a lucky streak a mile long or the grace of a gazelle as he hurdled one snare of roots after another. Once Clint broke free of the trees without somehow breaking his own neck in the process, he caught a fleeting glimpse of his quarry, just before the other man darted into another source of cover.

This time, it was a cluster of small shacks on the perimeter of the mansion. By the looks of them, the shacks were either servants' quarters or supply sheds. Clint didn't take the time to figure out which it was, since he was too busy trying to guess where the other man had gone after disappearing between two of the structures.

Clint slowed himself down as he approached the closest shed. Not too far away, there were sounds of heavy breathing drifting through the air. Sliding his finger over the trigger of his pistol, Clint worked his way to that shed and eased himself alongside its small, square-shaped window.

With his back pressed against the wall, Clint took one more step before turning on the balls of his feet and pointing his gun through the window. Although there was someone inside the shed, they weren't exactly the ones that Clint was after. Seeing as how the two people in there were tussling under the covers of a small bed, they didn't even notice Clint's sudden appearance.

Annoyed at the amount of time he'd wasted, Clint turned to put his shoulders once again against the wall. A flicker of motion from the corner of one eye was all the warning he got before something heavy was swung at his face.

Clint ducked at the same time as he brought his free hand up. He caught the incoming fist on the back of his own hand, sending it upward and past him so that the gun that the fist carried was smashed into the window, instead of Clint's jaw.

The man had snuck up on Clint like a snake in the grass and taken a swing using the handle of his gun as a club. That gun handle managed to connect with the glass pane of the window, which had been swung open to allow fresh air into the room. Although the couple inside the shack hadn't noticed Clint's prying eyes, they sure as hell noticed when the windowpane was noisily shattered into several pieces.

"Who's out there?" the man inside the shack hollered.

But Clint was too busy to respond. Even though his attacker still had his hand in the shack's window, Clint felt that man's knee come smashing up into his belly. It landed with a solid thump, and would have driven the air from Clint's lungs if he hadn't braced himself at the last possible second.

Clint tried to grab hold of the man's wrist, but couldn't get a grip on it, due to the awkwardness of trying to reach through the window. Just as his fingers started to slip around the man's gun hand, Clint felt that arm slither out of his grasp as the man took a few quick steps away.

By the time Clint adjusted his footing and swung his pistol around, his target was off and running once more.

Clint heard some more shouts as well as a few threats coming from the shack he had left behind. He was too busy running to bother with what was being said and soon the sound of that voice was lost amid the pounding of his own heart and the rush of breath through his lungs.

As he ran, Clint still saw the image of the other man's face. Indeed, that sight was burned onto his eyes, although he hadn't looked at the man's face for more than a second or two. The man had pale skin with sunken cheeks as well as a thick goatee, which covered his mouth like a bush. He also ran like a jackrabbit and was somehow managing to put even more distance between himself and Clint.

After hurdling a water trough, Clint raised his gun and took aim. "Stop running or I'll shoot," he shouted.

If the other man heard Clint, he wasn't about to follow the order he'd been given. In fact, he twisted around and fired off a quick shot in Clint's direction.

Clint didn't break his stride as he sighted down his barrel and pulled his trigger. The gun bucked in his hand and sent its fiery cargo toward the fleeing man in front of him.

Although Clint's bullet caught a piece of its target, it merely spun the other man somewhat like a target that had been grazed in a shooting gallery. Stumbling for a couple of steps, the man caught himself with both outstretched arms and kept moving on all fours until he righted himself once more.

"Jesus Christ," Clint swore under his breath.

Having wound their way through the shacks, Clint and the man he was chasing were now headed for the thicker mess of trees beyond the mansion. Unlike the trees in front of the large house, this greenery wasn't broken up by a trail or anything else. It was solid foliage, and the summer months had been awfully good to the thick, low-hanging branches.

Clint fired another shot, setting his sights just a bit lower than before. Although he couldn't tell if he'd hit the other man, he could see his target once again stumbling and fighting to regain his balance. Before that could happen, Clint fired again.

This time, the man dropped onto his side and rolled quickly into a sitting position. As soon as he'd turned himself around, he lifted his gun and pointed it at Clint.

There were no more than ten paces separating Clint and the other man now. That made it easy for Clint to see the wild look in the other man's eyes as he brought his gun around. Clint may not have known about the other man's skill with a pistol, but it would have been hard to miss from that distance, since Clint was still rushing straight toward that barrel.

Seeing that the man meant business, Clint threw himself to one side as the other man started pulling his trigger.

The gun let out a stream of thunder that sent angry hornets into the air all around Clint's head. As he was sailing toward the ground, all Clint could do was stretch out his arms and pray that he didn't get hit. Neither of those things failed him, since he managed to land without breaking anything or catching any lead.

Even before he'd stopped skidding in the dirt, Clint was firing at the other man. All he could hope for on that account was that his target hadn't moved since he'd started shooting.

But that wasn't the case. Not only had the man gotten his feet underneath him, but he'd also managed to scamper into the woods and disappear within the trees.

Clint got to his feet while emptying the pistol. He wasn't wearing his gun belt, however, so there were no rounds to refill the cylinder. He got to his feet and glared at the trees. Somehow, he managed to keep from tossing his gun into the woods out of pure frustration.

NINE

It felt like a long walk back to where Clint had left John and the others. Not only was he feeling all the twists and bumps he'd taken during the course of chasing down that last remaining gunman, but Clint was empty-handed. That last part stung more than any of the rest.

Even before he made it back to the clearing, Clint could see most everyone from the mansion and its grounds were milling about outside. Since most of the partygoers were clustered in a large, sequined group, the guards and their prisoner were easy enough to find.

"There you are, Adams," John said as he spotted Clint. "Where's that jackrabbit you ran off after?"

"Disappeared in the woods," Clint said with a shake of his head. "I would have gone after him, but—"

"No need for that," John cut in. "It was enough that you spotted him and chased him off before he took a shot at us."

"The hell it is," came another snarling voice that was all too familiar. Ed stomped forward with his hands on his hips and stared straight into Clint's eyes. "Why don't you ask that kid back there if it was enough?"

Clint met Ed's gaze without a flinch. "I did what I could."

"Yeah, well to hell with that!" Before Ed could say any more, he was stopped by a firm hand dropping upon his shoulder.

Keeping his hand in place, John moved Ed back a bit as he stepped in between the bigger man and Clint. "Ed's just spouting off, on account of what happened to the kid."

"I saw him by the senator," Clint said. "Looked like he was hurt."

"He's dead," John said simply. "Took a bullet through the head before we even got there." Looking over to Ed, he added, "Any of us."

Ed drew in a deep breath and finally lowered his eyes. He turned and walked back to the men gathered in a smaller clump nearby.

"What about the senator?" Clint asked. "Did he make it?"

"He's roughed up a bit, but he'll pull through. At least that's how it looks from what I saw. I ain't no doctor." John extended his hand with its palm up. "You still have that gun I gave you?"

Clint handed it over. "What the hell went on here? How did all of this happen so fast? I mean, those two were hardly gone for a minute or two before we knew something was going on."

"I can't say for certain, other than someone was after Senator Gray. As for the specifics, we're fortunate to have someone in our possession who should know a thing or two about the matter."

"One of those gunmen is still in one piece?"

John nodded. "And he's being wrapped up like a Christmas present as we speak. I figure on letting him stew for a little bit before I go in and pull some whos and whys out of him."

"I'd like to help out on that if I could," Clint said.

John was shaking his head even before Clint had finished speaking. "You were a hell of a help tonight, but this ain't your job."

"That speedy son of a bitch got away from me after leaving that dead guard behind him. I'll take part in straightening this out and won't hear anything to the contrary."

"I'm not even the one to decide such things, Adams."

"Then who is?"

"I guess that'd be that man right over there," John replied, while pointing toward another group of men dressed in fine black suits.

The man at the center of that group appeared to be in his late thirties and wore a closely trimmed mustache on a weary face. He was trying to speak to several politicians at once and doing a fairly good job of it. Despite the formal suit covering his stocky frame, he still wore a hat that would have been more comfortable on top of a man roping cattle.

"Who's he?" Clint asked.

"Name's Tucker. He's a United States marshal."

Clint nodded and committed the marshal's name and face to memory. After that, he looked back toward the spot where an older man and a few women were kneeling down and tending to Senator Gray. Not too far from that, a few more men were rolling a body wrapped in a tarp onto a stretcher.

"Get some rest, Adams," John said. "Have a few shots of whiskey and get to bed. All this will still be here in the morning."

"Is that what you plan to do?" Clint asked.

Without hesitation, John nodded. "Yep. And in that same order."

Suddenly, someone broke out of one of the larger crowds and came rushing toward Clint and the guards. All three of the men reflexively reached for their guns, but stopped when they saw Karen making her way to Clint with tears in her eyes.

"Oh, my Lord, are you all right?" she asked, while checking every bit of Clint that she could reach.

John started walking. Looking over his shoulder, he said, "Come back tomorrow, Adams, and I'll see about getting you involved in the cleanup. You've earned that much."

"Thanks. I'll see you then." Clint couldn't help but notice the grim look that was still hanging on Ed's face.

After a few moments, Ed nodded slowly and turned to head back toward the mansion. It wasn't much, but Clint had no trouble whatsoever in recognizing a silent apology when he saw one.

Clint was suddenly pulled in another direction as Karen took hold of his face and turned it so she could look at him straight on.

"Are you all right?" she asked again. "We heard shooting and then I couldn't find you and then I started hearing folks say that someone had been shot. It was terrible."

Slipping his arms up around Karen's, Clint took gentle hold of her face in much the same way that she was holding him. "I'm all right," he told her. "A little battered and bruised, maybe, but all right."

She seemed reluctant to leave it at that for a moment, but then she took a breath and looked into his eyes. After that, Karen wrapped her arms around him and melted into his embrace.

"It's been a long night," Clint said. "Let's get out of here."

TEN

The sun was still low in the sky when Clint made his way back to the mansion. As early as it was, there was plenty of activity around the place as well as the grounds surrounding it. The formal suits may have been missing, but the politicians and lawmen were still out in force. In fact, Clint was stopped by one of the latter even before he could get within throwing distance of the front door.

"Come back some other time," a stern sheriff's deputy said.

"I'm Clint Adams. I was here last night when the shots were fired."

The deputy wasn't impressed by that. In fact, he hardly even seemed to have heard it.

"Look," Clint said, "I'm expected."

"By who?"

It wasn't until that moment that Clint realized he had no idea about John's last name. The same went for Ed. Hell, he didn't even know the name of the kid who'd been killed. One name did spring to mind. Luckily, it was a good one.

"Marshal Tucker," Clint said. "He's expecting me, right along with the other guards who helped bring in that prisoner you've got."

The man at the door thought that over for a moment and then stepped aside. He also waved his hand to one of the other armed men nearby, who came striding over in response to the gesture.

"He'll take you to Marshal Tucker," the doorman said. "And if you're dropping names for no good reason, he'll take you out back and make you sorry you tried to step foot on this property."

"Fair enough," Clint said.

Although he kept a stern expression on his face while being led into the mansion, Clint wasn't so assured on the inside. By the reaction of the man at the door and the looks on the faces of all the men he saw inside the mansion, there was still plenty going on even after last night's shots had died away.

It might have been the same building that he'd been in the night before, but the difference between the mansion now and during the party was like night and day. There was no music and not a happy face to be found. While there were plenty of people about, every last one of them obviously had a purpose for being there, and they all glanced toward Clint with open suspicion.

Only when Clint was led into a small sitting room did he find a halfway sympathetic eye.

"Clint, you're here earlier than I expected," John said as he stepped over to greet him with a handshake.

"I almost didn't make it in at all," Clint replied. "The welcoming committee here isn't quite up to snuff."

"Don't feel bad. I got read the riot act myself and I'm supposed to be working here."

"I suppose I'm to blame for that," chimed in a man who'd been sitting at a small, rectangular table in the corner.

Clint recognized the man from the night before. Although the U.S. marshal wasn't wearing his formal suit from the ball, he was still wearing the same battered hat.

"Warren Tucker," the man said with a weary smile.

Clint shook Tucker's hand and found his grip to be strong and confident. "Pleased to meet you, Marshal. I'm Clint Adams."

"Clint Adams? 'The Gunsmith'?"

"One and the same."

"I've heard some stories about you, Adams. Even if half of them are true, you've got a lot to be proud of. Pleased to meet you, sir. Do you mind being called 'Gunsmith'?"

"I've been called worse. Actually, I'm still a gunsmith by trade, but some folks took to calling me that. I guess it's more colorful that way."

As Tucker broke off the handshake, he let out a tired breath and looked around at the rest of the room. "As much as I'd like to swap stories with you, we've got a bit of a crisis on our hands at the moment."

"I know. I was in the middle of it last night."

"And you have my thanks for that. Those killers caught me and a good number of my men with our britches down."

"I have a bad habit of being in the wrong place at the right time," Clint said. "Since I've made it this far, I was hoping to be of some help in straightening out whatever happened."

Marshal Tucker's smile was still tired, but was also very grateful. "Help of your caliber would be greatly appreciated. I'm going to need it since Senator Gray is only the first in a row of important government officials who've been set up for one hell of a fall."

ELEVEN

In the few moments it took for Marshal Tucker to send for a fresh pot of coffee and a cup for Clint, the number of armed men in and around the sitting room doubled. One of those new arrivals was Ed. The stocky guard stomped through the other lawmen like a bear through bushes and showed no sign of stopping until he got to John's side.

"Mornin', Adams," Ed grunted.

Clint tipped his hat. "You get some sleep or did you just take a shine to me in the last few hours?"

"Neither. What did I miss?"

"I was just about to bring Mister Adams up to speed on our situation," Tucker explained. "Would you like some coffee?"

"What I'd like is to know what the hell is being done about that murdering son of a bitch you got locked away upstairs."

"I wouldn't mind hearing that myself," Clint said.

"The prisoner is in custody and won't be seeing the light of day for quite some time," Tucker explained.

"Has anyone had a word with him?" Clint asked.

"He hasn't exactly been too cooperative, but it's early

45

yet. He'll loosen up once he realizes it's in his best interests to work with us."

Ed let out a discontented snort. "He won't say shit on his own. He knows damn well he's gonna hang or rot in a jail cell after what he done. Why would he talk, knowing that?"

"Because as far as he knows, there's still some light at the end of this tunnel."

With each second that passed, Clint found himself taking on more of Ed's harsh demeanor. "So that's it? You just let him think he can bargain his way out of this and wait for him to start talking? That's a little light, don't you think?"

"What would you have us do?" Tucker asked both Clint and Ed. "Should I string him up and torture him with hot coals?"

Clint held the marshal's gaze without so much as a flinch. "No, but there's got to be some middle ground in there. You must have done this before. Haven't you?"

"I'm not wet behind the ears, Adams, I assure you," Tucker said. "But this isn't exactly the normal situation."

Since the coffee had been brought into the room, John poured himself a cup and took a seat in one of the padded chairs along the wall. "Then why don't you tell us what the situation is, Marshal?"

"Gladly." Marshal Tucker poured some coffee and dropped in two cubes of sugar. "For the last few months, several high-level government officials have been incriminated in some crooked dealings involving several different areas of business."

Ed nudged Clint with his elbow and grunted, "That's fancy talk for some big rats in high places."

"Basically," Tucker said, "that's exactly right. Between you and me, there really wasn't anything too special about that. What is more unsettling is that these men were thought of as some of the finest elected into public office."

"Power corrupts," Clint pointed out. "Sad but true."

Nodding, Tucker sipped his coffee and said, "Right again, which is why these cases were handled like all the other charges of corruption. Things took a turn for the worse once these investigations all started pointing in the same direction."

"What direction would that be?" Clint asked.

"There have been several names mentioned, but all of these deals had some connection to a town named Harbinger. It's in Utah. Anyone ever been there?" When he asked that question, Marshal Tucker was mostly focused on Clint.

Clint thought it over for a moment and shrugged. "I could have passed through there, but I don't recall for certain either way."

The other two guards shook their heads.

"Well, there's a few men who've heard of Harbinger," Tucker explained. "And they're either dead or buried deep in a federal prison for crimes ranging from extortion to blackmail and murder. Every one of those crimes was committed against a judge, lawman or elected official."

"There have been elected officials murdered?" Clint asked.

"Only two so far," Tucker said. "But plenty others have died just for knowing or being related to one of those men. It seems that whoever is behind this uses threats of violence to sway his victims toward his line of thinking."

"And they all sound like some pretty influential victims."

"Yes, Mister Adams. They most certainly are."

The room got quiet for the next few moments as the marshal's words were digested. Apart from Clint, John, Ed and Tucker, there were three more armed men in the vicinity. Those others might as well have been statues, for the amount of expression they showed. Clint and the guards were taking on the same sense of being overwhelmed.

Letting out a breath, Tucker continued. "Last night's attempt on Senator Gray is the first time a man of his stature has been the target of an assassination. That means either Senator Gray has run afoul of a very dangerous man or he's being used as a way to influence somebody else."

"So how the hell are we supposed to know which it is?" Ed asked. "And how do we even know that it had anything to do with what you were talking about?"

"First of all, the way that Senator Gray was attacked was very similar to the way a federal judge in El Paso was attacked not too long ago," Tucker pointed out. "It was done with the same precision and under similar circumstances as this. Secondly, this isn't the first time that Senator Gray has been threatened."

"The kid mentioned something to me about that," John said. "He didn't go into any details, but he was spooked."

"Are you sure you didn't hear any more?" Tucker asked. "Part of why I wanted you all here was to go over facts like that."

John straightened up and lifted his chin just a bit. "That kid was good at his job. Part of that is to keep your mouth shut, rather than spill details in public that might put someone else in danger."

"Nobody's questioning his professionalism, John. We're just trying to put an end to this."

Sensing the friction on John's behalf, Clint decided to come to the marshal's rescue. "There's got to be more than those two things that make you think this is connected to anything else."

"There is," Tucker said. "The man we have in custody was spotted on two other occasions. Once in Dallas the night a mayor's aide was found dead after stealing some very delicate papers, and another time in Sacramento just before a few clerks from the capital went missing after doing their own share of damage.

"It wasn't until recently that enough of these crimes were connected that a task force was put together to deal with it. And this, my friends, is the best break we've had thus far. Normally, if anything is caught before the damage is done, it's just a few dead bodies and half a paper trail. Now, we've got a witness and a target that was kept alive, thanks to you gentlemen."

"It wasn't just us," John said grimly.

Tucker nodded. "I know. That young man last night wasn't the first to die while tracking down the root of this problem. My hope is that he's the last."

Finally, John eased up a bit.

"So what was last night about?" Clint asked. "Is Senator Gray the main target or was he being used to get to someone else?"

Tucker smirked. "That, Mister Adams, is where you come in."

TWELVE

"I got rights! You can't keep me here like this!"

As he shouted, the prisoner paced back and forth inside what would normally be considered a nice room. In this case, however, the room was looking more like a room in a mental hospital with every passing second. The bed had been turned over and all the linens had been scattered over the floor. The table and washbasin had been broken into pieces. All that remained fairly intact was a chair that had simply been tipped against a wall.

The man who'd done all the damage was the one who'd been captured in the clearing by Ed and John the night before. Apart from being red in the face from doing so much yelling, he looked like an average sort who'd had a bad night. Short, dark hair was sticking up from his head in odd places and his eyes had dark circles underneath them. His voice was hoarse and was even painful to listen to.

By this time, however, the guards seemed to have gotten very good at ignoring the prisoner altogether.

"You gonna take me to jail, then do it!" the prisoner yelled. "Just get me somewhere I can get to a lawyer and get me out of this goddamn room!"

Suddenly, the door swung open and one of the burly guards stepped inside. As always, the guard's face was a stony, unreadable mask. His shotgun was already at the ready and pointed straight at the prisoner's chest. After entering the room, the guard stepped to one side so Clint could walk in past him.

"Who the hell are you?" the prisoner grunted.

Clint nodded as he looked around at the mess. Finding the chair, he set it right and lowered himself onto it. "That's funny. I was just about to ask you that same question."

Although the prisoner had looked more than cocky at first, his smugness was fading fast. "I don't got to tell you a goddamn thing."

"True. But you might want to if you'd rather not end your life in a room much less pleasant than this one."

Clint could feel the prisoner's eyes roam over him, searching for anything useful. Just then, he had a real good idea of how a slow deer felt when getting singled out by a wolf.

"You ain't a lawman," the prisoner said. "Are you a lawyer?"

"Not hardly. And I resent the fact that you would accuse me of that."

"All right, then, smart-ass. Why the fuck am I even talking to you?"

"Because I'm your last chance to get out of this in one piece. You and the men you work for have pissed off some very powerful people. They're the sorts who can snap their fingers and make useless pricks like yourself disappear without a trace."

"And how do you know I'm working for anyone?"

"Because nobody smart enough to be in charge of anything would have gotten themselves in as much shit as you're in right now," Clint replied in a level tone.

The prisoner took that in for a few seconds. Even though he let some time pass to save face, it was plain enough that he was rattled by the deadly edge in Clint's voice. Also, his eyes kept searching Clint from head to toe, looking for something familiar or something he could work with. As much as he looked, he wasn't able to find a damn thing.

Clint had sat in on enough poker games to know when someone had reached the end of their rope. It was a feeling that every professional gambler got when he knew that only steam and desperate lies would be coming out of another player's mouth.

"You can't do shit to me," the prisoner said.

"Keep right on saying that to yourself," Clint said as he stared directly into the prisoner's eyes as if he meant to tear out the man's heart. "Maybe you'll be stupid enough to start believing it."

"Y-you were there last night," the prisoner said, with a sudden realization.

Clint nodded and forced himself to think about that young guard's face during their card game, as well as when he was lying in the dirt. He could feel the anger churning inside of him, and Clint knew well enough the prisoner could see it too.

"I'd start cooperating with us if I were you," Clint said. "Especially since we're so far away from anyone who gives a damn about you, and so close to a shed filled with a nice assortment of sharp tools."

"Someone get this asshole away from me! You get out of here right now or I'll take everything I know straight to the grave."

"So you do know something," Clint said. "That's a start. How about you tell me your name? What's the harm in that?"

The prisoner's eyes narrowed as he reflexively backed away a step or two from Clint. After glancing at the door and finding it shut tight, he let go of his bluster with a long exhale. "My name's Cam," he said in defeat.

"All right, Cam. How about you answer some questions for me?"

THIRTEEN

Clint stepped out of that room half an hour later. The guards kept their grim visages intact and stepped aside like two rock formations parted by an earthquake. The moment Clint was out, the door was slammed shut and locked. But all of that didn't even seem necessary this time around, since the prisoner inside made no attempt to get out.

After walking a few steps and turning a corner, Clint spotted Marshal Tucker, Ed and John waiting for him in the hall. Clint came to a stop and stood there with his arms folded across his chest.

"Well?" Ed asked. "Did you pull anything out of him?"

Clint kept his mouth shut for another few seconds as he shifted his eyes toward the marshal. Finally, he asked, "How did you know that was going to be so easy?"

Tucker shrugged and replied, "I didn't."

"I didn't have to do much more than go in there and say a few of the things you told me to. He didn't have much trouble believing that I was actually going to pull him apart with a pair of pliers and bury him in the backyard. After a few touches of my own, he started talking."

"Good. So our captive decided to cooperate."

"Oh, yeah. Cam couldn't talk fast enough before too

long. It got me wondering what the hell he knows about you marshals that I don't."

"It wasn't any real trick," Tucker admitted. "All I did was talk up the fact that we had someone here who was real good at causing pain and that he had a personal stake in what happened. You were a face he didn't recognize as one of my men, and you also happened to be at the ball last night. I'm just glad you agreed to go in there and play along."

Clint laughed a bit under his breath. "After a few minutes of seeing that man sweat in there, I almost started to feel sorry for him." When he saw the expressions on John's and Ed's faces, Clint added, "Almost."

Having already fished out a notebook and pencil from his pocket, Marshal Tucker flipped it open and started scribbling. "You said his name was 'Cam'?"

"That's right."

"Did you get a last name?"

" 'Wilson.' But I wouldn't put too much faith in that."

"Understood. What did he say about the attack on Senator Gray?"

"Just that he and the others were hired to do the job less than two days ago. But by the sound of it, it seemed that him and the others were just waiting to get that order anyhow."

"How many others?"

"He didn't say," Clint replied. "Tell you the truth, I don't even think he knew the answer to that one."

Ed let out a disgruntled sound that turned into a cough. "Why the hell wouldn't he know? He's in this up to his ears."

"Then why don't you ask Marshal Tucker exactly how many men are on the same payroll as him?" Clint asked.

As much as Ed wanted to get angry at that, he couldn't detect a bit of malice in Clint's voice. And when he realized that Clint had made a good point, he got even more frustrated. "Fine, then he's either holding out or there's more people in on this than we thought."

"We were hoping this was a tight-knit group with some big contacts," Tucker said. "But this might very well flesh out our biggest fear. If this is too big of a network, then it might not be long before any of what's happened here gets back to them."

"So nobody knows about this?" Clint asked.

"There was no way to keep the shooting secret, but I thought it would be wise to take advantage of the confusion and spread some rumors that could work to our benefit."

John nodded and looked at the marshal with new respect. "Good idea. What rumors are we talking about?"

"First off, as far as folks know, Senator Gray died of his wounds earlier this morning. Secondly, the man we have in custody has escaped to parts unknown. He was wounded as well."

"Good thinking," Clint said. "That should buy some time before the men he would report to get too suspicious."

"And," Tucker added, "there's always the possibility that he died somewhere along the way, before reporting to anyone. Did you get any more out of our prisoner, Mister Adams?"

"It was a lot of bits and pieces, but I'm sure that Senator Gray wasn't the only target in his sights. This came when he was getting his nerve back, but he kept talking as if he'd done what he wanted and it was too late to stop the rest."

Ed smiled and said, "And if there's more to be done, then there's still a chance to put a stop to it."

"Exactly."

It took a moment, but soon Ed's face was as grim as everyone else's. "But . . . we still don't know what it is that needs stopping."

"Exactly. All I got in that regard was that there was something in the works that even the fear of God wouldn't have gotten Cal to talk about. And believe me," Clint added, "I gave it one hell of a try."

Marshal Tucker took off his hat and ran his hand over

the top of his head. The summer heat was permeating every bit of air inside the mansion and it couldn't be felt any better than on the upper floor where they all happened to be. "I need to make some arrangements to move the prisoner," he said. "As much as I'd like to make good on some of Clint's promises, we need to ship Cal to a prison where he'll be spending the rest of his life. Why don't we meet up in an hour?"

Everyone nodded their agreement and started heading for the stairs. After John and Ed had gone down to the main floor, Marshal Tucker stopped Clint by putting a hand on his shoulder.

"I've truly heard some good things about you from some very reliable sources," Tucker said. "And I was wondering if you truly wanted to make good on that offer to help out in this."

"Whatever you need," Clint replied.

"Good. Head out to the stables and get your horse ready. Someone else will be riding with you. The two of you need to ride as soon as possible."

"Where am I going?"

"Harbinger, Utah."

FOURTEEN

This time when he left that mansion, Clint finally felt as if he was getting away from all the chaos surrounding the place. Compared to that big house swarming with lawmen of all shapes and sizes, the rest of the town seemed downright tranquil.

Clint's first stop was the hotel where he was staying. When he walked up to the front desk, he was greeted by a friendly, yet very surprised, clerk.

"Mister Adams? You're still here?"

Making a show of looking himself over and then glancing back to the short clerk, Clint nodded to the middle-aged man and said, "Appears that way."

The clerk let out a flustered laugh and said, "Of course it does. I just thought you'd already moved on."

"I'm not the sort to skip out on paying for my room."

"The bill's settled," the clerk said as he turned the register around so he could run his finger down the page. Before too long, he nodded and smiled. "Yes, sir. Paid in full."

Even though Clint took a look for himself, the ink on the register didn't do much to alleviate his own confusion. "What about my things? I've still got some bags in my room that need to be collected."

"That's already done, as well."

"When did this happen?"

"Not too long after you left this morning."

Clint stood there for a moment, exchanging curious glances with the clerk. Since that wasn't accomplishing much, he started to leave. He stopped at the last moment, turned around and asked, "I wasn't the one who did all this, was I?"

"No, no. It was one of the U.S. marshals. They showed me a badge, so I let them pay your account. I thought you already knew about it."

"I do now. Mind if I take a look to make sure they didn't miss anything?"

"Not at all!"

The clerk unlocked the door to Clint's room. All it took was a minute of poking around for Clint to see that the only things in there were what had been there when he'd first arrived. With nothing else left for him to do, Clint tipped his hat and left. He made it about two paces outside the hotel when he saw Karen Vatterov hurrying down the boardwalk.

The moment she spotted Clint, Karen broke into a run and practically leapt into Clint's arms.

"Oh, thank God you're all right," she said. "I've been trying to find you ever since last night."

"I'm fine, Karen. It just looks like I'll be leaving town pretty soon."

"How soon?"

"Probably within the hour."

"Can you tell me anything about what happened?" she asked. "I know you were involved in the shooting, but I haven't been able to find out anything more than that."

"It's not that I don't trust you, but there isn't much to say. I'll tell you what I can when I get back, all right?"

She nodded and gave him a kiss that lingered just long enough to remind Clint about the events just before the previous night's ball. When she pulled back, Karen was wearing a sneaky little smile.

"I wasn't too surprised to hear that you were in the middle of all that when the shooting started," she whispered. "Being around you, there's never a dull moment."

"Likewise. Did you manage to get your own business concluded?"

She nodded.

Clint winked at her and said, "You might want to steer clear of that sort of thing for a while. This town's crawling with federal lawmen now."

Suddenly, the smirk on Karen's face vanished. "What? Did they ask about me? What did they say?"

"I'm sworn to secrecy. How about you just stick to running your saloon and leave the other deals under someone else's table where they belong?"

Once most of the panic had left her eyes, Karen shrugged. "I guess my place is doing plenty well enough to stand on its own. I can do without paying the governor any more visits."

"Good. I'll pay you a visit the moment I get back into town."

"You'd better, Clint Adams. The governor isn't the only one I've got dirt on, you know."

Clint kissed her and waved his farewell while heading down the street. That didn't leave much else for him to do besides head to the one spot he was told to go to.

FIFTEEN

The stables weren't too far from Clint's hotel. In a matter of minutes, Clint had rounded a corner that put the barn-sized building in his sight. As he pushed open the smaller door cut out of one of the large main ones, he half expected to find the stall where he'd left Eclipse just as empty as his hotel room.

Not only was the Darley Arabian stallion right where he was supposed to be, but there was also a familiar set of saddlebags propped up against the stall's door.

"You're a sight for sore eyes, boy," Clint said, as he stepped up to Eclipse's stall and held out his hand. "Nobody came along to bother you, did they?"

Although the Darley Arabian sniffed at Clint's hand, Eclipse shot a few nervous glances toward another section of the stables. Clint picked up on the signal immediately and spun around to get a look behind him.

There was indeed someone behind Clint, but it wasn't exactly the type of someone he'd been expecting. Even so, Clint kept his eyes peeled and his hand directly over the modified Colt on his hip.

"Who are you?" Clint asked in a calm, no-nonsense tone.

The person who'd come up behind Clint was a woman almost a full head shorter than he was. Her golden hair hung loosely over both shoulders and was held away from her face only by the battered Stetson she wore as if she'd been born with it on her head.

Her skin was tanned to a color just shy of cinnamon and was smooth as silk. The clothes she wore weren't anything special. They were just a dark blue shirt with the sleeves rolled up, tucked into a pair of form-fitting jeans. Even if she wore a burlap sack tied by a rope around her slender waist, the tight curves of her body would have been difficult to miss.

Raising her hands to reveal the double-rig holster around her waist, she took a step forward and stopped. "My name's Tara Locke. I take it you're the one and only Clint Adams?"

"If I was performing in a circus, maybe. Out in the world, I'm just Clint Adams."

She smirked at that and started to come closer. Pausing while glancing down at Clint's gun hand, she asked, "You mind if I put my arms down?"

"Only if you tell me where you came from."

She lowered her arms and hooked her thumbs behind her belt. "Sorry about that. I wasn't supposed to draw much attention until we left town."

"We're leaving town?"

"Isn't that why you came for your horse?"

"Yeah, but I was thinking that I'd be on my own, or maybe meeting up with someone along the way."

"You are meeting up with someone," Tara said as she flashed Clint a pretty smile. "Me."

Clint didn't mind taking in the sight of her for a few moments as he decided what he should or shouldn't say.

As if reading the dilemma etched on Clint's features, Tara said, "Marshal Tucker told me to meet you here. I'm also the one who had your things collected and brought over from the hotel."

"Oh, that was you, was it? Well I don't exactly appreciate feeling like I'm being rushed out of town."

"Time is of the essence, Clint. I'm sure you know that."

"I'm not a marshal, but isn't there something I need to see or hear before I trust you? For all I know, you could be working for the wrong folks."

Tara leaned forward and met Clint's gaze. "We're headed for Harbinger, Utah, on a matter concerning a threat to several government officials. This is in connection to the shooting last night and has ties to several judges across the country that—"

"All right," Clint interrupted. "You've got me convinced. Just so you know, all I wanted to see was a badge."

Having frozen where she was, Tara looked away from Clint as a bit of red flushed into her cheeks. "Right. A badge." As her head drooped a bit, she reached for the bandanna tied around her neck and turned it over. Sure enough, there was a small U.S. marshal's badge pinned there. "How's that?"

"Good enough for me," Clint replied.

In a matter of minutes, both of their horses were saddled up and ready to go. Tara left some money to cover the costs for both stalls and was just about to ride out when Clint moved in front of her.

"Let me go first," he said.

Her eyes narrowed a bit as she replied, "I'm supposed to be your partner. Surely Tucker told you to expect someone else along with you. If you have a problem because I'm a woman, then you'll just have to—"

"I don't have any problem of the sort," Clint interrupted. "In fact, I quite like women. I just thought that since you went through so much trouble in trying to keep hidden, we might not want to ride down Main Street side by side on our way out of town."

Slowly, Tara started to nod. "Good point. You go on ahead."

"You sure about that?"

"Yes. Just go on ahead and I'll catch up to you a mile north of town."

Clint could feel her starting to bristle and decided against needling her anymore. He did have to admit that she had a cute way about her when she got flustered. Since he didn't have any time to think too much about that just now, Clint snapped his reins and rode out through the stable's front doors.

After winding through a few crowded streets, Clint gave Eclipse a nudge, which was all the stallion needed before speeding up. As the buildings began to thin out and the land opened up in front of him, Clint became aware of someone following him.

It wasn't Tara.

SIXTEEN

There were two of them that Clint could see. As much as he would have been happy to have just those two after him, Clint knew better than to get his hopes up like that. When someone decided to rush up on someone from behind, they turned out to be a lot like rats. There were always plenty more lurking around than the one that could be seen right away.

Clint snapped his reins and hunkered down over Eclipse's back. Fortunately, it had been a while since the Darley Arabian had stretched his legs, so the stallion was more than happy to run faster. Before he let Eclipse go full out, however, Clint held off and allowed the riders behind him to tip their hand.

There was always the possibility that they were simply headed out of town at the same time he was.

There was the possibility that they were just two friends out for a ride to exercise their horses.

Those men could have lived outside of town.

And there was always the possibility that they were getting their guns out of their holsters just to take a look at the craftsmanship that had gone into creating the weapons.

"Damn," Clint said under his breath as he turned and

saw that both of the riders behind him had not only drawn their weapons, but were taking aim at him.

The pounding of hooves against the dirt was getting louder as the riders dug their heels in and raced to catch up to Clint. Along with the slap of leather against horse-flesh, the sounds of gruff voices were also starting to drift through the air.

Clint took another quick look behind him as well as a look to either side. In a matter of seconds, he figured the riders would be close enough to start firing. Not only that, but Tara was nowhere to be seen. At least he didn't have to wait long before he found out how much of a help she was actually going to be.

Just as he'd figured, Clint heard the first shot not long after he turned to face front once again. The bullet hissed in his direction, but was high and to the right. Another shot quickly followed and, by the sound of it, had been fired by a different gun than the first. That one missed as well, making Clint feel better about the quality of marksmen he was dealing with.

Clint patted Eclipse's neck and tugged the reins a bit. The stallion was plenty used to the sound of gunfire, but was itching more than ever to break into a full gallop. "Easy boy," he said. "Let's reel them in just a little bit more."

Eclipse took well to the sound of Clint's voice and obeyed every touch of the reins as more lead flew past him.

Clint wrapped the reins around his left hand while reaching down with his right. Once he found the rifle strapped to the side of his saddle, he kept his hand in position while pulling Eclipse into a quick turn to the left.

Sure enough, when Eclipse veered from his course, another series of shots cracked through the air. As soon as he heard one shot from each of the different pistols, Clint pulled the rifle from its holster and levered in a round.

By the time the rifle was ready to fire, Clint had twisted

in his saddle and was sighting along its barrel. He fired one shot before his eyes even had a chance to fully focus on his targets, aiming low and in the middle of both riders. The bullet drilled a hole in the ground at the horses' feet, kicking up just enough dust to get into both animals' eyes.

Suddenly, the riders had their hands full with just trying to keep their horses from splitting off and heading off the trail. The animals didn't panic too much, but the brief respite was more than enough for Clint to lever in another round and draw a bead on his target.

The rifle bucked against Clint's shoulder once more. This time, he knew his bullet would hit home even before he saw one of the riders jerk back in his saddle. Clint watched for another second until that same rider managed to pull himself back into position and slow his horse down. The man's gun had fallen from his hand and his arm was hanging limp at his side, which was exactly what Clint had been after when he'd pulled his trigger.

That left only one other rider to worry about before Clint was free and clear. Suddenly, that train of thought was broken up by the sound of more gunshots coming from somewhere in the distance to Clint's left. When he shifted around to get a look in that direction, Clint could only make out a few dust clouds being kicked up. A shot from behind him reminded Clint that he still had some business that needed to be wrapped up.

Touching his heels to Eclipse's sides was all that was needed to get the Darley Arabian charging. The stallion raced forward with his legs tearing up the ground beneath him.

Clint reflexively adjusted to Eclipse's movements and hunkered down low. Soon, he pulled the reins and turned Eclipse to the right while also bringing the stallion to a stop. His heart was slamming in his chest and his breath was burning in his lungs, but Clint managed to steady himself just enough to take another shot.

A few more gunshots cracked through the air, but Clint ignored them. When he lined up the shot he'd been waiting for, Clint squeezed his trigger and felt the rifle buck against his shoulder.

This time, the bullet hissed so close past the approaching horse's head that the animal reared and pumped its front legs into the air. Although the rider did a good job of hanging on, he wasn't able to keep his wits about him when another shot came from Clint's rifle and clipped him just enough to make him lose his grip on the reins.

The moment he saw the rider start to topple to the ground, Clint snapped his reins and got Eclipse moving again. They got to the other frightened horse while its rider was still writhing in pain on the ground.

Surrounded on all sides by at least half a mile of open land, Clint could see that there were no other members in this ambush. The shots in the distance had died off as well, so Clint took his time and got up close to the man who'd just managed to flop himself onto his back.

SEVENTEEN

Letting out a few strained breaths, the man on the ground reached down to feel the jagged bone protruding from his knee. The moment his fingers felt that wet protrusion from the tear in his jeans, he let go and flopped onto his back.

Another horse was approaching and was already getting close enough for the fallen man to hear the animal's breath. When he looked for his own mount, he realized he was even farther away from it than he was from the pistol, which had slipped from his hand upon impact.

Gritting his teeth, the rider sat up and turned to see Clint looking down at him from his saddle.

The horse's eyes were wide and near panic, but Clint's bullet had only left the animal with a shallow cut along its neck. It ran off a few paces as Clint drew closer, but didn't bolt far from where its rider had fallen.

"Son of a bitch!" the rider shouted. "My leg's busted!"

"Could have been a whole lot worse if my aim wasn't so good," Clint replied.

Turning his head to spit, the rider glared back up at Clint. "You barely hit me! Even that was probably nothin' but luck!"

As Clint swung down from Eclipse's back, he kept the

rifle pointed at the man beneath him. "Actually, you're the lucky one, since I wanted to have this little chat with you rather than just blast you straight off your horse and into hell."

"F-fu—" the rider started to say. He stopped the moment he saw Clint's boot lower to within a hair's breadth of the bone sticking out of his knee.

"Ah, ah, ah," Clint warned. "I'd watch the language if I were you."

Just looking at the fallen man's leg was enough to make Clint's stomach clench. Even if the rider had been shooting at him moments ago, Clint couldn't bring himself to actually step on the poor bastard's shattered knee.

Of course, there was no need for the rider to know about Clint's little dilemma.

Bending his upper body down without actually moving his boot an inch, Clint made it look as if he was lowering himself straight onto that gnarled mess of blood and bone. "Why were you trying to shoot me?" he asked.

All of the fight drained from the wounded rider, along with the color from his face, when he saw how close Clint was to stepping on his broken leg. "All right, all right," the rider said in a breathless rush. "Me and a few others were sent for anyone who talked to that U.S. marshal."

"Which marshal?"

"I don't know." When he saw Clint ease himself down a little bit more, the rider stuck out both hands and waved them as quickly as he dared. "I swear, I don't know the name! All I know is it was some marshal. One of the others with me pointed him out and then said you was the one we needed to shoot."

Clint let it go at that, confident that the rider was too panicked and talking too quickly to make up a lie that would have been halfway convincing. "How many others of you are there?"

"Four." Glancing in the direction that his partner had

gone after nearly being knocked from his own saddle, he added, "Three, now that that asshole went off and deserted me."

"Where are the others?"

"They went after somebody else."

"Who?"

"I don't know." Before Clint could say anything or move a muscle, the rider spat out, "I swear to God, all I know is that it was someone else. I don't know his name, but it was someone who was there when Senator Gray was shot."

Clint eased his foot back. Even though his boot hadn't so much as touched the other man's knee, he saw the rider on the ground exhale as if he'd just survived a day's worth of torture.

"Anything else you want to tell me?" Clint asked. "Considering how badly you need to see a doctor, getting on my good side might be a very smart idea right about now."

"Just that I hope you track Vernon down and gut him like a pig for taking off on me like that."

"Vernon?"

The rider nodded. "He's headed for Utah and will probably be staying at cathouses along the way. He'll hole up in those before he makes camp or even steps into a hotel. And don't worry about that being a lie, since that chickenshit took off even though I know he had another gun to replace the one you made him drop."

The fact of the matter was that Clint didn't have one bit of trouble believing the wounded man on that account. He could see the anger in the rider's eyes, which told him he probably could have gotten that bit of information out of him without any coercion whatsoever.

Clint walked back to Eclipse to remove his bedroll and some bandages from his saddlebag. "Here," he said placing the bedroll within the rider's reach. "Lay back and don't do anything stupid."

"What the hell?"

"I'm just going to wrap that leg a bit so you don't bleed out." Clint had already draped some bandages over the man's broken knee. Although it didn't look pretty, it was enough to staunch what little bleeding there was. He was done before the rider had a chance to ask another question.

Clint got up and climbed back into the saddle. "Stay here and I'll send help for you. It shouldn't take long, since we can still see town from here. And I'd advise against trying your luck in getting away," he added while taking up the reins. "That is, unless you fancy the idea of hacking off your own leg or dying from gangrene."

Those last few words put a fearful look in the rider's eyes. Letting out a disgusted grunt, he lay back on Clint's bedroll and gritted his teeth. When he bothered looking for Clint again, he found nothing but dust swirling in the air.

EIGHTEEN

Even though Clint wasn't about to leave a man to die alone in the grass with a broken leg, he also had another priority that was higher on his list. Thinking of that rider that had been shooting at him not too long ago, he knew that Tara might very well be shot or in some other danger at this very moment.

The shots he'd heard a little while ago were long gone, but Clint knew well enough where they'd come from. Snapping the reins against Eclipse's flank, Clint hung on as the Darley Arabian raced in the direction from which those other shots had come.

Before too long, he spotted another horse winding its way through a patch of trees. As he pulled back on Eclipse's reins, he realized that he'd already been spotted by whoever was on that horse. Clint took the rifle from its spot along his saddle and laid it across his lap. Although he wanted to be ready for another spot of trouble, he didn't want to invite it by waving a gun around without good cause.

Before too long, he flicked the reins again and got Eclipse moving to meet up with the other rider that much quicker. The second horse emerged from the trees and waited patiently for Clint to arrive.

"Are you all right?" Tara asked as soon as Clint was close enough to hear her. "I heard shooting."

"So did I. Did you get ambushed on your way out of town?"

"Not exactly, but I did see someone get in the middle of a scrap before riding off. He headed north and was chased by at least two others. I started to follow, but turned back rather than leave you on your own."

"I appreciate the concern," Clint said. "But I managed to hold my own."

"You were attacked?" she asked while riding up so she could get a closer look at him. "Did you get hit? What happened?"

"I made it through just fine. There's at least one man who needs some medical attention, so why don't I tell you about the rest on our way back into town?"

"Who's hurt?" Tara asked.

"One of the men who attacked me broke his leg," Clint replied while steering Eclipse toward town. "Come along and I'll tell you the whole story."

Clint filled Tara in on all the important details of what had happened after they'd parted ways at the stable. It didn't take long for them to ride back into town, find a doctor and tell him where to pick up the man with the busted leg. After that, Clint and Tara left once more and headed north.

"You're not still worried about folks seeing us together?" she asked.

Clint shrugged. "After what happened to me, I'd say that whoever was interested in anything like that was already watching close enough to figure out whatever they needed."

"Good point."

"Did you manage to get a look at who was being shot at before they all rode off?" Clint asked.

Tara shook her head. "Not really. By the time I got there, I spotted a few unfamiliar faces that were doing most of the shooting. There was one other farther up who was doing a hell of a job dodging the bullets, but he was a ways off from me." Suddenly, she snapped her fingers and added, "There was one other fellow who cut through the middle of it all. The shooters seemed to recognize him, but he just kept on going as if his tail was on fire."

"My guess is that'd be Vernon," Clint said.

"Vernon? Oh, right. The one who got away."

"I did my best to keep those men alive, but didn't expect that first one to turn tail and run so quickly."

Smirking, Tara said, "I've seen plenty of tough talkers bolt as soon as a few shots get too close to them."

"Yeah, but with this much at stake, the hired guns tend to have a little more sand than that."

Tara nodded, but eventually said, "It really doesn't make much difference now, anyway. I mean, he got away, didn't he?"

Clint looked over to the blonde who sat easily in her saddle, swaying slightly as her horse carried her along. "He got away because I thought you might be in trouble," Clint said.

"All right."

"Sounds to me like there's something else you wanted to say."

Although she didn't deny that, Tara gritted her teeth and stared straight ahead while she mulled some things over. Finally, she let out a breath and turned to face Clint once again. "There is something else I wanted to say."

"Good thing we've got a ride ahead of us," Clint replied. "That means plenty of time to talk."

"It took me a long time to get where I am. It took me

more time than you could imagine just to get a badge pinned to my shirt, not to mention get a spot in the U.S. marshals. That bunch of old boys don't take too kindly to women wanting to join up with them."

"I can imagine," Clint said earnestly.

"No matter how many times I've proven myself, I always get stuck with the jobs that either amount to nothing or are some tiny bit of what's really going on. Since riding with you seems to be one or the other of those two things, I'd appreciate it if you just stay out of my way and try not to let any more potential witnesses ride off."

"Whoa there!" Clint said in a way that made both Tara and Eclipse come to a stop. "I could have shot both of those two men dead the minute they started shooting at me. But I kept them alive and even got some information out of one of them."

Tara brought her horse around so it was standing side by side with Eclipse. Not only did she stare straight into Clint's eyes, but she didn't even flinch when he raised his voice. "And I suppose you couldn't have gone after him once he rode off?" she asked. "Sounds to me like he's more valuable than the one whose leg you broke."

"I didn't have to do any of this, you know. I wanted to lend a hand because I knew I could help. If you'd rather work alone, then just say the word, lady."

"Oh, I wouldn't dare let the great and mighty Clint Adams go anywhere without being there to witness the event."

Although Clint had something in mind to say to that, it only took a moment for him to realize how stupid they both sounded right about then. When he allowed himself to smirk, he saw the anger grow even hotter in Tara's eyes.

"What's so funny?" she asked.

"I was just thinking. I'm known as a gunfighter who tends to be mixed up in more than anyone has a right to be and you're a sharp-tongued woman doing a fine job in a man's field. Is it any wonder why Tucker put us together like this?"

"You mean besides making sure we were pestering each other so he could catch a moment's peace?" she asked, without being able to keep her own smile from showing.

After a few more seconds, both of them started to laugh.

"I may be outspoken sometimes, but Tucker's not the sort to send someone out to get hurt just so he could be rid of them."

"I got that feeling too," Clint said. "Which means he must think we can do some good out here. How about we get back to it?"

She reached out and shook Clint's hand. "Agreed."

They started riding north again. This time, however, they did so as true partners.

NINETEEN

The satchel flew through the air and landed with a soft thump on the top of an old table. Although he sat in a wobbly chair in a dark corner of a dirty saloon, Zack gazed out at the world as if he was its master. His bony fingers were steepled in front of his face as his sharp eyes flicked over the faces of the two men standing in front of him.

"Who the fuck are you two?" Zack asked.

While both of the men had walked in strong, they shrank back a little when they felt the edge in Zack's voice.

"We brought your money," one of the men replied. He was clean-cut and had what most folks would consider to be a hard face. Compared to Zack Richards, with his venomous eyes, he could very well have been a choirboy.

Zack leaned forward and grinned. "Do I need to count it?"

The clean-cut man and his slightly rumpled partner both shrugged silently. Their hands went reflexively for the guns at their sides.

Zack nodded and picked up the bag. "I think I should count it." As he pulled the drawstring and stuck a hand inside the pouch, he looked away from the other two across from him, as if the men had simply stopped existing.

"You boys wonder why I let you in here wearing those guns?" Zack asked.

The sudden discomfort on both of the other's faces revealed that they hadn't exactly thought about that.

"It's because I admire a man with guts," Zack said, in answer to his own question. "It also shows me that Senator Grinbee must be expecting trouble for him to send you two rather than come here himself. Tell you what," he said as he took one hand from the pouch. "If I come up short, I'll let one of you take the blame and the other walk out of here alive. What do you say?"

Just then, four of Zack's hired guns emerged from the shadows or stood up to walk over from other tables. After a few nervous glances, the two messengers realized that there were more like four hired guns assigned to each of them.

"We're just supposed to deliver that," the first messenger said.

Zack shrugged and got back to his counting. Before too long, he'd removed all the bundles of money and arranged them before him. Looking back up to the messengers, Zack picked up the pouch, turned it over and shook it.

"It's short," Zack announced.

The second messenger shifted on his feet, unsure of whether he should go for his gun or run for the door. Opting for neither, he said, "Grinbee said he couldn't get it all in time. That's all he could manage."

When Zack nodded at the messenger who'd just spoken, it was with a cordial smile. "Thanks for your candor. That just fixed one decision for me." He then looked to the first messenger and said, "Shoot your partner there now and you can leave here to tell the senator what a mistake he made."

The clean-cut man not only looked at the gunmen closing in on him, but at the rest of the saloon. It wasn't the biggest or fanciest place, but it was full of people and teeming with all sorts of activities one might expect in such a setting. There were card games being played, drunks swapping jokes and even working girls making their nightly rounds.

"You wouldn't shoot anyone in a crowded place like this," the messenger said.

The second messenger was no longer able to put words together.

"You have that much faith in your fellow man?" Zack asked. "You think any of these good folks are stupid enough to step in on account of you two?"

Before either of the messengers were able to make a sound or move a muscle, Zack reached down and plucked the Smith & Wesson from the holster strapped over his belly. The gun was a bulky model and oiled to a glistening sheen, but neither of the two messengers could get much of a look at it before the weapon spat at them with a tongue of smoky flame.

There was a low thump, which quieted every sound in the saloon.

Soon, a weak groan could be heard as the second messenger reached for his gut and found a warm puddle of blood soaking through his shirt. From there, he dropped to one knee and grabbed the side of Zack's table to keep from falling over.

With a look from Zack, the rest of the saloon got back to its own business.

"It'll take him a while to die," Zack said to the remaining messenger. "You do me a favor and I'll see he's put out of his misery."

The messenger's face was pale as he looked down at his partner, who was gasping for air and slowly sinking to the floor. Gritting his teeth, he started reaching for his own gun. He didn't even get halfway before his wrist was grabbed by one of the other gunmen and the weapon was stripped from its holster.

"Your heart's in the right place, kid," Zack said. "That's why I like you. I want you to take a message back to Senator Grinbee."

"A . . . message?"

"That's right. Do that and I'll see to it that your partner here doesn't feel any more pain." When he heard the wounded man let out an agonized wail, Zack flashed another grin. "I wouldn't think too long about it if I were you."

"Fine. What's the message?"

"Tell him he can have his money back. We're going the other route. He'll know what that means."

"Anything else?"

"Yeah," Zack said as he stood up. "Tell him that if he fucks around with me this time, I won't be nearly so generous. Now get out of my sight."

The messenger started to leave, but didn't take more than a few steps before looking back to his wounded partner. "What about him?"

Zack put one hand flat against the table to support himself as he leaned forward. He then reached out with his other hand to point the gun down at the man on the floor and pull his trigger. "Take him with you." Coming around the table, Zack holstered his gun and removed a long, slender knife from an inside pocket of his jacket. "Well, you'll be taking at least a bit of him with you."

TWENTY

Senator Grinbee sat across from Zack Richards at that same table less than ten hours after the blood was mopped up from the floor. Perched on the edge of his chair with his hands folded on his lap, he glanced around nervously, as if he expected doom to come at him from any angle at any moment.

"I-I can get the rest of your money," Grinbee said. "But I told you before that it was going to take some time."

Zack was in the same chair he'd been in the night before, but this time he was playing solitaire and sipping from a cup of hot tea. Without even looking in the senator's direction, he shook his head. "Too late for that."

"But you . . . you kept the deposit I sent."

"I sure did. But . . . didn't you get my message?"

The senator quickly averted his eyes and swallowed hard. When he spotted the dark stain on the floor under his own chair, Grinbee felt a cold sweat break out upon his brow. "Yes," he replied with a nod, while still keeping his eyes away from Zack. "I got your message."

"Then you must know that I don't want your money anymore. I want you to start working for me."

Grinbee shook his head. "I can't do that. I just . . . can't."

Zack's voice became an icy dagger which cut straight through the senator's chest. "Oh, you'll do whatever the hell I tell you to do. Especially since you're connected to the assassination of one of your esteemed colleagues."

As Grinbee's eyes snapped up to look at Zack, he leaned forward, as if he'd been struck on the back of his head. "What?"

"Don't you recall our earlier conversation?"

"You had Dan killed?" Grinbee looked around in a panic, but was unable to find a single sympathetic face. "You couldn't have done that! He wasn't a part of this! That's impossible!"

Zack merely shrugged and flipped over another couple of cards. "I warned you about this. Since you knew what might happen, you're the one who got him killed."

"So he's . . . dead?"

"Yeah. He's dead."

"Oh my God," Grinbee moaned as he pressed his fingers to his temple and slumped back in his chair. "Oh my God."

"You want some time to pray or would you like to get back to business? From what I hear, the law's all over Senator Gray's death like flies on shit and it won't take them long to find out where you fit into this. I'll see to that personally."

Dropping his hands into his lap, Grinbee shook his head and asked, "What do you want from me? What can I possibly do for you that won't ruin my career in the process? There isn't a single favor I could grant that would actually be carried out before I was run out of office and prosecuted. Surely you understand that."

"I understand more than you know about politics," Zack replied. "In fact, I know so much that I've learned that so much more can be accomplished sitting outside the game than tossing my hat into the ring."

Flipping over another card and placing it onto the layout in front of him, Zack casually shifted his eyes between his game and the sweating senator across from him. "You see, dirty little men like you aren't too hard to find. You're more than willing to commit your sins and push your luck, because you think you'll never get caught. But do you know what I hate more than anything else in this world?"

Although he didn't have enough air in his lungs to speak, Grinbee shook his head.

"What I hate more than anything else is dumb bastards who actually do get lucky and make it to the top when their rightful place is at the bottom. Gamblers are good for that, but they don't last long. Politicians, on the other hand, stick around for years after pulling off a miracle and strutting around like everything was their own doing."

"I don't . . . understand," Grinbee squeaked.

"Of course you don't. You just went about your life trying to do good and pleasing the people who were good enough to vote you into office."

Zack's eyes fixed upon Grinbee. The moment he saw Grinbee start to nod, Zack slammed his fist upon the table hard enough to make every one of his cards jump. "Bullshit!" he snarled while stabbing a finger into Grinbee's face. "You barely even know what you're signing, thanks to the opium you toss down your throat. And you hardly make it into any of the meetings you're supposed to attend, because you're fucking so many young girls who get tricked into coming into your room. And do you think all those bribes you've been taking are such a big secret?"

The color drained from Grinbee's face, but he'd looked like death warmed over ever since he'd arrived in Harbinger. His eyes jostled back and forth in their sockets as if he was reading a newspaper and his lips trembled as though he was reciting a speech.

"You want to know the only thing that surprised me?"

Zack asked. "That you were too damn stupid to pay me off before it came down to this."

"I can get you the money," Grinbee said quickly. "I can get it for you tomorrow. I swear to God."

"Not interested. The only redeeming quality with assholes like you is that you're all so predictable. Thanks to a long string of men like you, I'll practically be able to pass my own bills into laws. You've got some work ahead of you, but not as much as it may seem. You're just a simple piece of a bigger machine, which is the way it should have been the whole time. Only this time around, you're part of a machine that will actually function."

"And what if I say no?" Grinbee asked in a voice that wasn't much more than a pained groan.

"You recall what happened to that man I sent back to you?"

Reflexively, Grinbee's eyes darted toward the blood-stained floor and a shudder worked its way through his body. "Yes."

"I can make that look like a picnic and it's a picnic that you'll be on with your family and a few other of your friends that I've got my eyes on."

Grinbee let out a tired breath. "What do you want me to do?"

TWENTY-ONE

Spotting Vernon's tracks wasn't difficult. All Clint and Tara needed to do was revisit the spot where she'd seen him ride past, and then look for the tracks that connected that spot to the place where Clint had been ambushed. The fact that Vernon's horse had been running made the job that much easier, since the prints in the ground were deeper and there were that many more broken branches and twigs to show the way.

The tracks joined up with a broken-down trail heading north. Without being led to that trail, Clint might not have ever found it on his own. Fortunately, that meant that hardly anyone else used that trail either. Vernon's tracks were so easy to follow that they might as well have been colored with red paint.

"Should we get moving faster?" Tara asked. "We might be able to catch up to him."

Clint was down on the ground to make sure they were still following the correct set of tracks. Pressing his hand against the ground, he traced one of the indentations there and looked ahead. "By the looks of this, I'd say he was still pushing that horse of his as hard as he could when he came by here."

Tara looked back and then down at the tracks. "He was still at a full gallop? But this is half a day's ride from where we started."

"That's my point. If he's been moving that fast for that long, we won't catch up to him by trying to outrun him."

After a few moments of silent thought, Tara grinned and said, "There's a town not too far from here. In fact, this trail takes up pretty close to it."

"How big is it?"

"Big enough to have someone there selling horses or a blacksmith to look after one that threw a shoe."

Clint stood up and nodded. "That's exactly what I was thinking. If Vernon's pushing his horse this fast immediately after riding hard to catch up with me, he should be running into a problem or two fairly soon."

"And considering how panicked he was back at the ambush, I'd say he's not even thinking clear enough to give that poor animal of his a rest. If he hasn't been through this next town, he'll likely be at the one after it."

"I like the way you think," Clint said as he climbed back into his saddle. "We'll keep following these tracks and see where they lead. If they're heading toward that town, we can make a race of it."

With a snap of leather, both of them were off and running once again. The summer was being kind to them by keeping the air warm but not unbearably hot. The sun was beating down from the blue sky, but the trail was mostly covered by a canopy of leafy branches. All in all, Clint couldn't have asked for a nicer day to ride, and Eclipse was happy as ever, being able to stretch his legs and run to his heart's content.

Now that they had a travel plan, neither of them were in a particular hurry to cover ground. Unlike the man they were chasing, Clint and Tara switched between riding at a run and a walk. Soon, they could hear the distant sound of running water.

"How about we steer toward that stream?" Clint asked. "I hit bottom on my canteen a while ago."

But Tara wasn't as eager to steer away from their course. In fact, she had yet to take her eyes off the trail or acknowledge that she'd heard a word Clint had just said.

Although he tried to follow her line of sight, Clint couldn't see anything more than dirt and fallen leaves. "What's the matter? You see something?"

"Maybe," Tara said as she brought her horse to a stop and swung down from the saddle. Crouching down low, she crept toward the side of the trail as if she was sneaking up on a small animal.

Only when Tara squatted down next to a patch of flattened grass did Clint see what had caught her eye.

The dirt had been kicked up in that spot fairly recently and clumps of grass had been dug out and tossed farther into the trees. The closer he got, the more tracks Clint spotted. First, there were just erratic prints left by a horse kicking and fussing while turning in a circle. Then, a little farther off the trail, boot tracks joined the horse as the rider obviously got off and calmed the animal.

But Tara was moving toward something else. Reaching out with a smile on her face, she picked up a piece of iron that was sticking partly out of the ground. Once she had it, she stood up and held it out for Clint to see. The end of the iron piece was shinier than the rest, since that was a part that had been freshly broken off.

"Remember when I said something about his horse throwing a shoe?" she asked proudly.

"Damn," Clint said as he looked over the chunk of broken horseshoe for himself. "You're good."

TWENTY-TWO

Finding that horseshoe was both a blessing and a curse. For one thing, Clint knew that it was too much of a coincidence for tracks that fresh and iron broken that recently to belong to anyone else besides the man they were after. There was always the possibility that some other unlucky rider had left that iron, but Clint knew in his gut that wasn't the case.

It told them that Vernon's head start was diminishing quickly and that he would most definitely be headed for that town to get back on track once again. But there was another side to all that good news.

Now, Clint and Tara couldn't move along as casually as they'd been going before. Now that he was riding on a horse with a wounded hoof or worse, Vernon would be twitching at every snapping twig and looking twice at any shadow that might possibly be someone closing in on him.

Of course, there was always the possibility that Vernon was going under the assumption that nobody was on his tail, but Clint wasn't feeling that lucky.

Since they'd discovered the spot where Vernon had been forced to dismount and tend to his horse, Clint and Tara had been moving at a snail's pace. They also hadn't spoken more than three words to each other and had come to rely on a set of hand signals so they could keep their ears open for any sound they could hear.

Clint led Eclipse by the reins as he stuck close to the tracks that Vernon had left behind. That way, he could make his best guess about how fresh those tracks were and where they were headed. Behind him, Tara rode holding a spyglass to her eye so she could look for any sign of Vernon or his wounded horse.

Finally, Clint stopped and hunkered down to get a look at something in the grass. When he was done examining it, he motioned for Tara to come up close to him.

"What did you find?" She asked.

"Some horse droppings. I'm not expert enough to tell much from them, but they're awfully fresh. I'd say he couldn't be more than a mile ahead of us. Maybe less."

Tara let out a low whistle. "Jesus, he must have been flying to get that far ahead with a wounded horse and all."

"The important thing is that he won't be flying anywhere now. Which way to that town?"

After taking a quick look around to get her bearings, Tara pointed a little to the right of the direction in which they were already facing.

"Good," Clint said. "That's the same way the tracks are headed. He must be going there."

"If we catch up to him before he gets there, we can get him without a horse and without anywhere else to run."

"True, but he'll also be desperate. Not to mention the fact that he's got to be looking for trouble coming from all sides. If we wait until he's in town, we might be able to swoop in and catch him once he's let his guard down."

"What's the matter, Clint?" she asked. "I thought you were a hell-raising gunfighter."

"And I thought you were a peace officer. Sounds to me like you're itching for a fight."

"I just like the odds out here where there's nobody else

around. If something starts up in town, then innocent folks might get caught in the cross fire."

Clint thought it over for a second and nodded. "Good point. Since you're the marshal here, I'll leave it up to you."

"All right, then. We'll fan out and cover as much ground between here and—"

Suddenly, Tara was cut short by the sound of a gunshot in the distance. Although both of them crouched reflexively, there was no hiss of lead through the air to mark a bullet coming their way. Instead, they heard the pained whinny of a dying horse.

"Sounds like our friend has just been slowed up a bit more," Tara said.

"Can you see them through that spyglass?"

Tara pointed the telescope toward the sound of the gunshot and squinted through the lens. Before too long, she nodded and whispered, "I can't be certain it's him, but there's someone up ahead and he doesn't look too happy."

After a few more seconds, a smile grew upon Tara's face. "Oh, it's him all right. I'm just surprised we can't hear him swearing from here."

"What's he doing?"

"Stripping off what he needs from his horse."

"Good, then now's the time to get him."

Tara collapsed the telescope and stuffed it into her saddlebag. "Right. You head off that way, and I'll go around the other way so we can catch him in the middle. Just remember one last order from Tucker."

"Another order from Tucker?" Clint asked. "What's that?"

"No matter what that man does or what he pulls, he needs to be brought in alive. That is, unless we can guarantee on finding someone else who'll know half as much as he does."

"I figured that much on my own," Clint said as he settled into his saddle and checked over his Colt. "But that still leaves us some latitude in how healthy he is when we hand him over."

"Sure. But don't forget, it's alive or nothing on this. And by nothing, Tucker means that's how much understanding he'll have if we lose this witness."

"I'll try to keep that in mind once the shooting starts." And with that, Clint snapped his reins to get Eclipse moving.

Tara brought her horse around to face in the opposite direction before touching her heels to the animal's sides. In the stillness that followed, the echoes of a man swearing profusely drifted through the air.

TWENTY-THREE

Vernon was limping around on his left leg, gritting his teeth and shaking his fist in the air. It might have been a funnier sight if his other fist wasn't wrapped around a .38 caliber pistol. Every so often, he would punctuate a particularly nasty curse by pointing his gun at the dead horse lying nearby.

"You goddamn nag! Can't even take me from one place to another? What the fuck good is a horse who can't fucking run?!"

Now that he had that out of his system, he stepped over to the saddlebags which were lying over the horse's side. Everything from that bag had been taken out and tossed onto the ground. Bending down, Vernon took hold of the bag and tossed it over the horse. The bag on the other side was wedged underneath the dead animal and wouldn't budge no matter how hard Vernon pulled on the free end.

"Son of a . . ." Vernon grunted as he dug in his heels and pulled with every bit of strength he had. ". . . uhhhh BITCH!"

As that last word came out of his mouth, Vernon's fingers slipped from the saddlebag and he toppled over backward. Even though he flailed his arms like a turkey trying to fly, he still managed to land on the same rock sticking up from the ground that he'd hit the last time.

Vernon jumped to his feet and felt pain shoot through his hip. It didn't last as long as before, since the second blow seemed to have numbed him a little. That numbness lasted right up until he turned and kicked at the rock in a fit of rage.

His toe slammed against the rock and crunched within his boot, since that rock didn't so much as budge under the assault.

"Having a little problem there, Vernon?" came a voice from the surrounding trees.

Immediately upon hearing that, Vernon lifted his pistol and fired a shot toward the voice. His eyes darted nervously as he tried to find out where the voice had come from.

"Who's there?" Vernon shouted. "Come on out. I won't shoot."

There was a rustle behind him, but by the time Vernon spun around to look, he found himself staring straight into Clint's face.

"What the—?" Vernon hollered as he reflexively shuffled away from Clint.

Clint kept his hand over his holster as he said, "Drop the gun, Vernon. You're not going to get away from me this time."

"Holy shit," Vernon groaned. "It is you!"

"It sure is, now drop the gun."

"I'd do what he says," Tara said as she rode up and drew her horse to a stop. Not only was she in perfect position, but she already had her rifle aimed at the squirming fugitive.

"Who's the lady?" Vernon asked.

"She's the one with the rifle on you," Clint replied. "So I'd be sure to treat her real nicely."

"Oh, I will." With that, Vernon twisted around to point the gun at Tara. Just as he was about to take proper aim, he felt Clint's boot smack down against the foot that had been repeatedly slammed against that half-buried rock.

Although the curses swam through his mind, Vernon was in too much pain to let any of them out. Instead, all he could do was bite down on his lip and clench his eyes shut as the agony tore through him. As soon as the pain in his foot became a little easier to bear, he decided to do his best to kill both of these new arrivals.

Unfortunately for Vernon, Clint had already stripped him of his weapon.

"Come along with us, Vernon," Clint said while tucking Vernon's gun into his belt. "And if you behave like a good boy, I might give you something to take an edge off the pain of those broken toes."

"My toes ain't . . . broken," Vernon wheezed as he tried to take a step without using the hand Clint was offering. He made it about half a step before he was too dizzy to go on.

Clint holstered the Colt and draped one of Vernon's arms across his shoulders. He then lifted Vernon the way he would help a drunk walk down the street. "You've got some fire in you, Vernon. I'll give you that much."

"Where are you . . . taking me?"

"There's a town nearby. We'll head there to get something to eat and some rest. After that, you're going to tell the U.S. marshals everything you know about what the hell was going on with Senator Gray."

Vernon's skin was already pale enough. He didn't exactly look sick, but more like the sort who just didn't take well to the sun. His cheeks were sunken in a way that made it clear he was always a skinny little cuss. Pointed cheekbones poked out to accentuate his narrow nose. A thick patch of bristly hair surrounded his mouth and covered his chin in a mediocre attempt at a goatee.

As pathetic as Vernon may have looked before, all that turned around when he started struggling against Clint with a wild look in his eyes. "You ain't taking me to no federals! If that's the case, you might as well shoot me now!"

"They're taking you into custody," Clint said as he dragged Vernon along, despite the other man's kicking and screaming. "There isn't much to do about it now."

"They'll execute me!" Vernon screamed. "Since you haven't done that by now, that must mean you don't know who you're dealing with!"

"And I suppose I should just listen to every word you have to say because you've got my best interests at heart," Clint said as he helped lug Vernon over to where Eclipse was waiting.

"Yeah," Vernon said quickly. "Well, I see why you'd be suspicious, but I got no reason to lie to you. I'm already caught."

Clint took the rifle from his saddle and tossed it over to Tara. She caught it and holstered it in her own saddle as Clint climbed onto Eclipse's back. Reaching down for Vernon, Clint said, "You've got plenty of reasons to lie to me, Vernon. Don't treat me like an idiot and I'll do my best to get you into town without dropping you on your head."

"But, I know things! I can make it worth your while. Just give me a chance!" And Vernon babbled on and on like that, pleading for mercy even though he didn't so much as lift a finger to him throughout the entire ride into town.

TWENTY-FOUR

Clint didn't catch the name of the town as he rode into it. He was more focused on trying to block out Vernon's constant chatter, which switched between begging for his freedom and complaining about his foot. Tara rode behind them, keeping her rifle aimed at Vernon's back while trying not to laugh at Vernon's continuous, inane babble.

Holding his Colt in hand so Vernon couldn't get to it, Clint had to fight the urge to use the gun just to get the man behind him to shut his mouth for a few seconds. By the time they found a hotel, he was kicking around the notion of using the gun on himself just to get a moment's peace.

"Stay here," Tara said as she tied her horse outside the hotel. "I'll go in and get us some rooms."

"Be quick about it," Clint said.

"And make sure I've got a comfortable bed," Vernon added. "I got a bad back."

"Shut up, Vernon."

After a few minutes of blissful silence, Clint saw the hotel's door swing open and Tara walk out.

"I got us two rooms," she said. "And I explained our situation, so we won't have to be subtle in locking up our guest."

97

"Two rooms?" Clint asked.

"I figured one of us should stay with him. I mean, we can't just leave him to his own devices."

"Yes, you can," Vernon said while nodding vigorously. "I swear I won't—" All he needed was the stern glare from Clint to shut his own mouth and look away.

Shifting his eyes back to Tara, Clint said, "You can stay with him. Since he'll be chained to something either way, it won't make any difference who else is in there."

"Well . . . I wasn't sure that would be . . . proper."

"Oh, because you're a woman?" Clint asked. Rolling his eyes, he let out a sigh and said, "And you wonder why other marshals don't like being assigned to you."

"That wasn't nice," Vernon said.

Now it was Tara's turn to glare at the prisoner. The anger in her eyes shut Vernon up even faster than when he'd gotten stared down by Clint.

"Fine," she snipped. "He'll bunk with me and you can sleep with your horse for all I care."

Tara pulled Vernon along and it was all he could do to keep from breaking his neck as he slid down from Eclipse's back. His hands had been tied somewhere during the ride into town, so she took hold of the rope around his wrists and used it to lead him toward the hotel.

"Here," she said while tossing something toward Clint. "Your room's next to mine. You think you can manage taking the bags up or should I do that too?"

Clint caught the key and began unloading the horses.

Tara stomped into the hotel, dragging Vernon along behind her.

TWENTY-FIVE

A little later, a knock sounded on Tara's door. She walked to the door, pulled it open and frowned at who she saw in the hallway.

"Oh," she grunted. "It's you."

Clint leaned against her door frame wearing the best smile he could manage, considering how tired he felt. Rather than say anything just then, he took the arm that had been behind his back and brought it around to reveal the little bouquet of flowers in his hand.

Tara looked at the flowers and back at Clint with the same expression of cool disinterest. "What're those for?"

"They're for you," Clint replied.

"And does this go back to me being a woman? You think you can toss some flowers at me and I'll just melt?"

"Well, you're partly right. If you were a man, I'd buy you a drink. Either way, I'm just trying to apologize for how I acted."

Although she did a good job of hiding it, Clint could see something close to a grin struggling to come to the surface. Even so, she had yet to take the flowers from him.

"Mind if I come in?" he asked.

She stepped aside and walked into the room. "We're partners, Clint. No need to be so formal."

The room was slightly bigger than Clint's. There was a good-sized bed along one wall and a large chair beside the window. A table and washbasin were on the other side of that window. The room's most striking feature, however, was the little fireplace on the wall adjacent to the door. Actually, the most striking feature was the man chained to that fireplace.

Vernon's hands were no longer tied together with rope. Instead, his wrists were manacled together and the chain of those manacles was looped through a curve of steel which was part of the fireplace's decoration. Having his arms stretched over his head made Vernon look like a fish dangling from a low hook. He sat with his back to the wall and his legs splayed in front of him. His face was as anxious as ever.

"Those are pretty flowers," Vernon said. Looking to Clint, he winked and added, "Nice touch."

Stepping in and shutting the door behind him, Clint tossed the flowers onto the small dresser against the wall closest to the bed. "There's a restaurant just down the street. It's getting late, so we might want to head over there before it closes."

"I thought you said you've never been to this town," she said.

"I haven't. But I'm sort of in the habit of picking out places to eat whenever I ride into a place for the first time. I'd bet whatever they're serving there is better than what we could get here. What do you say?"

Clint could read Tara's face well enough to know that she was interested. At the last minute, however, her stubborn streak reared up and sank its teeth in.

"I can't leave here," she said. "Not while I need to look after my guest over there."

Looking over to Vernon, Clint shrugged and placed his

hand upon his Colt. "Then I can just shoot him in a leg or two. Or maybe I'll just put one in his head and say he was trying to escape."

"Aw, Jesus!" Vernon shouted as he started flailing and jerking like a fish on the end of a line. "Aw no! Jesus!" As he sputtered, Vernon tried to get to his feet, slipped, and tugged with every bit of strength he had against his manacles and the iron loop set into the wall.

After he'd seen enough, Clint gave Vernon a smirk and said, "He's not going anywhere. You did a fine job of locking him up and that piece of iron is probably anchored to the foundation of this building."

Having frozen in mid-squirm, Vernon waited a few more seconds before relaxing again. "You're a sick man," he said to Clint. "That was a hell of a thing to do."

"I'll make it up to you by bringing you a steak. Sound good?"

Sitting back down again, Vernon shot Clint a spiteful glare. "Medium well."

"Medium well it is." Clint held an arm out for Tara. "Shall we?"

She let out a sigh and made a show of pulling herself to her feet. "I guess I might as well, since you're obviously not going to leave me alone anytime soon."

Although she walked next to him after locking the hotel door behind them both, she didn't take the arm that Clint offered. Even so, her mood was growing lighter with every step they took down the hall. By the time they stepped outside onto the darkened street, she was nearly back to her old self.

"We shouldn't be out long," she told him. "Lord only knows what that weasel is capable of."

"Vernon's a runner. If he couldn't get away when he thought I was going to shoot him, he won't be going anywhere. Besides, you wouldn't have left that room if you weren't sure of that very same thing."

Slowly, Tara nodded. "True."

"Sorry I snapped at you earlier. It's been a hell of a long couple of days."

"Yes, it has." Tara shrugged and looked directly at him for the first time since their spat had started. "I guess I've had more than my share of men talk to me like that. It's a pretty sore spot with me."

"Now I know."

"So where's this restaurant you spotted?"

"Right down the street." As he turned a corner, Clint pointed to a small storefront halfway down the block. There was a faint light still glowing in the window and a single, hand-painted sign that only had one word on it: STEAK.

"That's the place that caught your eye with a fleeting glance from fifty paces away?"

"That word always catches my eye. Let's eat."

TWENTY-SIX

"Wake up."

Vernon felt a nudge, rolled as much onto his side as he could and resumed snoring.

"I said, wake up."

When he heard that, Vernon groaned, opened his eyes a crack and saw someone reaching down for him. Seeing that unexpected motion was enough to jostle him out of sleep and get him fighting against his manacles one more time.

"Relax," Clint said as he reached down to set a plate next to Vernon. "It's just the steak I promised."

Vernon watched Clint set the plate down and place a spoon and butter knife on its edge. "How am I supposed to eat when I'm tied to this damn fireplace?"

"Simple. We're going to take those manacles off." With that, Clint stood up and stepped back so Tara could use her key to unlock the manacles. Clint's hand never strayed from his Colt and his eyes remained fixed upon Vernon the way a bobcat watched its next meal from the branches of a tree.

The manacles came off without incident and Vernon

lowered his arms with a pained wince. His arms flopped onto his lap like dead weight. By the time the blood was flowing through them properly once more, Tara had taken the manacles away and stepped back. Clint was seated on the edge of the bed.

Poking at his steak with the utensils he'd been given, Vernon held up the spoon and rounded knife. "How the hell am I supposed to eat a steak with these?"

"It's a good steak," Clint replied. "You'll manage. If not, I wouldn't mind taking it for myself."

"Nah," Vernon grunted as he pushed the meat down with his spoon and started sawing with the butter knife. "I'll make due."

"I thought that you might." Clint waited until Vernon devoured his first few bites before talking again. "How about a little dinner conversation?"

"How about you leave me in peace?"

"How about for dessert I shove my boot down your throat?"

Vernon froze with a hunk of steak halfway to his mouth. The cocky expression slowly melted away as he shrugged and said, "Fine, then. Go ahead and talk."

"What I'd really like to know is who wanted Senator Gray dead."

"Who?"

Leaning forward a bit, Clint slammed his boot down so hard that Vernon almost dropped his spoon.

"I didn't get no names," Vernon said.

"You just took an order to kill a man and didn't ask any questions?"

"Yeah. A man tends to stay alive longer without asking questions."

"Who else was with you that night that Senator Gray was shot?"

Vernon shrugged. "I was just supposed to give you some

grief when you rode out of town. I don't know much about the rest."

"I know you were there, Vernon. You ran off like a scalded dog just like you did when you tried to ambush me." Leaning forward a bit more, Clint added, "One of your friends back at the Governor's Ball told me it was you that ran off. Next time you stab a partner in the back, you should make certain they're dead."

If Vernon had any hopes of lying about that again, they were dashed by the guilty look on his face when he heard that. He did his best to cover it with a scowl and got back to his food. "So I was there. That ain't no secret."

"The question is why you were there," Clint pressed. "Who sent you?"

Vernon was scared. He was nervous. He was also very determined to keep his mouth shut regarding this particular subject. The only time he opened his mouth was to shove in a piece of roughly cut steak.

Clint kept his eyes focused on Vernon and could feel the tension growing thicker between them. Most of that came from Vernon's attempts to keep quiet while also trying to maintain a tough look.

Behind Clint, Tara watched Vernon as well. It was she who broke the uneasy silence. "That's it. If he's not going to help out, then there's no reason to keep him around."

"Stop it, Tara," Clint said, without taking his eyes from Vernon. "We talked about this."

"Yeah, we talked, but that doesn't change anything. You remember what our orders were. Dead or alive. If he's just going to be a load for us to drag around, then there's no reason for us to feed him steak."

"I'll get paid more if he's alive," Clint said.

"You'll get paid plenty. I'm sure Senator Gray's family will pitch in enough to make it worth both of our whiles to just drop this miserable toad right here and now."

Vernon's eyes twitched between Clint and Tara. Although he gripped his spoon in one hand, he seemed to have lost his appetite during the heated exchange.

"I'm not going to kill this man in cold blood," Clint said.

Tara took up her rifle and levered in a round. "Then you can leave the room. I'll do it, but that means you'll have to be the one to carry the body."

Clint got to his feet and looked back to where Tara was standing. When he shifted to look down at Vernon, he shrugged and said, "That sounds fair."

"Wait a second!" Vernon spat. "I can tell you some things. It's just that none of it will do you any good."

"Shut up," Tara growled. "I'm sick of your double talk."

Vernon raised both hands to cover his face, sending the piece of steak on his fork over his shoulder, where it slapped wetly against the mantel. "The man you want is in Harbinger, Utah."

"I know that much already," Clint said.

"Fine, fine. Umm . . ."

"What's the man's name?"

Vernon sucked in a breath and literally chewed on his tongue.

"Step aside, Clint," Tara said while sighting along her rifle. "I don't want to get any blood on your boots."

"Zack Richards!" Vernon squealed. "For the love of God, his name's Zack Richards!"

"What does he want with Senator Gray?" Tara asked.

"There's some other politician in Harbinger that Zack is trying to get on his payroll. In a day or two, there's some stories set to be published in some newspapers that will tie in that politician with the men that killed Gray."

"You're certain about all that?" Clint asked.

Vernon nodded from behind his upraised arms. "Me and the others I rode with dropped them stories off on our way to kill the senator and ambush you."

"Where were they dropped?"

"All over. Some in Texas, one in Santa Fe, and some others in Nevada. We've been riding and delivering that shit for weeks. I even got bored enough to read them damn articles a dozen times."

"That's a lot of trouble to go through to get a senator in your pocket," Clint said. "What's this Zack Richards need with him?"

"It's not just that one senator," Vernon said. "I've made runs like this plenty of times. Zack's got enough politicians under his belt to run this country. I know 'cause I been there to deliver the things that put them in Zack's pocket."

"Deliver what kind of things?"

"You name it. Letters, photographs, documents. I've sneaked into more places than I can count and it wasn't to steal anything but other bunches of papers or such. This is the first time I been in on a killing."

"Promoted, huh?"

Vernon looked up at Clint, but quickly looked away. "Yeah. Something like that."

"Seems like you made a real mess of it."

Although Vernon didn't respond with words, the heavy sigh that seeped out of him told Clint more than enough.

"I may not have met this Zack Richards fellow," Clint said, "but my guess is that he's not going to take too kindly to hearing that you ran off after botching an ambush and got yourself captured. He'll like it even less when he hears about all you've said to us here in this room."

Vernon's eyes snapped open wide. "You can't let anyone know about this! They'll hurt me bad."

"I bet they will. Especially when they see you with us riding into Harbinger."

"I can't go to Harbinger. Not like this!"

"Then you'll have to work with us," Clint said. "Tell us all we need to know so we can get in there nice and quiet and get back out again without raising too many suspicions."

Once again, Vernon glanced back and forth between Clint and Tara. Eventually, he started to nod. "I'll do it. Not like I got any other choice."

Clint smiled. "You might not be as dumb as you look."

TWENTY-SEVEN

Harbinger was a town that looked like it had been built from driftwood. Every structure was blackened and leaned to one side or another. Any breeze at all would set loose a trail of dust from any number of rafters or knock free a board which swung noisily from a rusty nail. The odd thing about it was the amount of people still living in a place that seemed as if it had already been abandoned.

Like many other towns that had sprung up fast and managed to stay alive, Harbinger was a tough place out of sheer necessity. So many other places had fallen under their own weight that just about any town needed strength or money in order to survive.

Thanks to Zack Richards, Harbinger had both.

In a town like Harbinger, men like the well-dressed gentlemen walking down Main Street were easy to spot. Despite the guns on their hips, those men still looked more likely to disappear than stir up any sort of trouble. Even the drunks lying in the gutters regarded them as prey.

One of the men walked ahead of the others. He carried a satchel under one arm, which he seemed to regard more highly than the gun around his waist. He was tall, with narrow features, and had a droopy face, despite the fact that he was obviously not an old man. His chin was immaculately shaved and every hair on his head was in its place.

Walking beside and slightly behind the first man was another who was dressed similarly, but carried himself much differently. He wore the same suit of clothes, but the holster he wore seemed to fit better around his waist. It was tooled and well worn. The gun inside of it was never more than an inch or two from his right hand. He had the eyes and walk of a predator hiding in the body of a dandy.

There was one other gentleman with them who looked to be the age and type who belonged in a suit. The gun he wore was clean and new. To the narrowed eyes watching the gentlemen from all angles, the weapon was purely for show and not doing a very good job of it.

The gentlemen stepped into the saloon on the corner, which was marked with just the number four drawn on the wall. It was a bright day, but none of that sunshine made it through those doors. After a few moments, the gentlemen's eyes had adjusted to the shadows and they spotted the smiling man beckoning to them.

"Come on inside, fellas," Zack Richards said with an enthusiastic wave. "Have a drink."

Two of the gentlemen stepped forward, leaving another one behind them. "We didn't come here to drink," the man in front said. "We just came to deliver this."

With that, the gentleman at the back of the group extended an arm to hand a satchel to the spokesman. The one who'd done the talking so far opened the satchel and removed a bundle of papers. "I'll need you to sign these."

Zack took the papers and flipped through them in a rush. After glancing at a few elegantly scribed words, he cheerfully tossed the papers back.

"I'm not signing these," Zack announced.

"You need to in order to make this official."

" 'Official'? Who sent you here? Was it Beatty? That fat bastard's been trying to wiggle out of our arrangement since it started. You boys go back to Salt Lake and tell your boss that I'll contact him when I need him. It doesn't go the other way around. You should know that by now, Beakman."

"I may still be working for Beatty, but that won't be for much longer. By the way, I intercepted some more letters linking the state's treasurer to a group of crooked cattle barons."

Zack shook his head. "I wish more higher-ups were like Beatty. They make it so easy for me. I'll take those letters, but I hardly need them. So these papers aren't just another offer to pay to get me out of what's left of Beatty's hair?"

"No. Those papers are the ones you've been waiting for since you hired me."

"Already?" Zack asked as he snapped the papers up again. "They're two weeks early."

"Well, they need to be signed if you want to move up the political ladder. I think you should give them another look."

Zack looked the papers over one at a time. This time, however, he read each one even more carefully, until a sly grin crept onto his face. "This is some fine work, Beakman. Are these documents the genuine article?"

"No, but they're close enough to do the job. Actually, the only other person who could tell the difference is dead."

"I can't have my name in writing on something like this."

"You'll need to, in order to withstand any scrutiny that might be turned in your direction. From what I understand, you're almost far enough along to take the next big step. Is that right?"

Zack nodded.

"When you do that, you'll need to step forward as Zack Richards and not some shady character using a false name. Do that any other way, and you'll be ripe for picking from anyone else using the tactics to which you are so familiar."

"I never thought of it that way."

"Sign those papers and you're an officially recognized judge. It doesn't matter who says what about you, they won't be able to take that away."

"That is, if someone's stupid enough to say anything."

"That's your concern."

"It certainly is." Grinning from ear to ear, Zack took a pen and signed his name to the documents. When he handed them over, he said, "You're doing a fine job, Beakman."

"Thank you, sir." Accepting the papers, Beakman turned and headed for the door. He stopped after a few steps and looked over his shoulder. "I should say, thank you, Judge Richards."

TWENTY-EIGHT

After Vernon had finished his steak, he wasn't in the mood to talk any longer. In fact, he barely said two words the rest of that night and the following day. Even as he sat behind Clint with his wrists manacled and his arms behind his back, the prisoner didn't do anything more than shift every now and then to maintain his balance.

Clint had no complaints about this arrangement. On the contrary, it was actually a fairly pleasant ride.

"I need to stop," Vernon croaked.

Clint looked around, as if the voice had come out of thin air. "Did you hear something, Tara?"

She smirked and looked over at them. Even though she'd ridden beside Clint this entire time, the sight of Vernon slouched over on the back of Eclipse's saddle never stopped being funny. The prisoner had a way of looking like a poor, wilted flower, even after having tried to ambush Clint a few days ago.

"I do believe our guest said something," Tara said.

Clint grinned. "And here I thought he was mad at us."

"Yeah, yeah," Vernon replied. "Just stop, will ya?"

"Why?"

"Because I need to."

113

"Need to what?"

Letting out a sigh, Vernon said, "I need to take a piss. Jesus Christ, you barely let me out of your sight since you started dragging me around like some kind of dog."

"Am I supposed to feel sorry for you now?" Clint asked. "Because if that's what you're trying to do, it's not going well."

"I could always just piss right on this horse," Vernon grumbled.

"Do that, and I'll let him return the favor." Just as he started to hear genuine whining from the man behind him, Clint tugged on the reins and brought Eclipse to a halt. "Just make it quick," he said, while pulling Vernon down from the saddle.

Clint took hold of Vernon by the arms and brought him down, as if he was unloading a sack of grain from the back of a wagon. He wrapped one arm around the man's back to keep him steady as Vernon struggled to get both legs under him. When he took his arm back, Clint felt something warm and wet on his hand.

"What the hell?" Clint groaned as he took a look at what was smeared on his fingers. Part of him was relieved by what he saw. Blood was a whole lot better than the other possibilities. After a split second of thinking along those lines, he heard alarm bells clanging in his head.

Letting out a vicious snarl, Vernon used every bit of the strength he'd been gathering to pull both arms to his sides. Blood had covered his hands and soaked into the manacles to make them just slick enough for him to get his wrists through. It took a lot of effort and opened a nasty gash on both hands, but Vernon got one wrist free.

"Yeah!" Vernon shouted as he swung an arm around in a half circle. That arm had the chain still dangling from it, which connected solidly on the side of Clint's head.

Clint had started to move out of pure reflex, but the impact of the manacle and chain sent a dull wave of numbing pain through his skull. One moment, he felt like his face was cracking open and the next moment, he felt nothing at all.

As soon as Clint stumbled back against his horse, Vernon ducked and ran for the bushes along the side of the trail. A shot exploded from behind him, putting an extra bit of steam into his steps.

"Goddammit," Tara said as she levered a fresh round into her rifle. She barely even remembered taking the weapon from the holster on her saddle, but was swearing at herself for not drawing it fast enough to hit Vernon before he scampered off.

"You all right, Clint?" she shouted.

Although Clint heard a voice that might have been Tara's, there was still a bit too much fog in his brain for him to know what she'd said. As he tried to shake some sense into himself, he saw a bleary picture of Vernon's fleeting back. When he felt something touch his shoulder, the surge of adrenaline sharpened his focus.

Clint's instinct was to protect himself against another attack. It took no time at all for him to see that it was Tara who had come up beside him.

"Are you all right?" she asked again, quickly.

To Clint, it felt as if hours had dragged by since Vernon had hit him. Since he could still see some branches shaking in the other man's wake, he realized he still had plenty of time to catch up to him.

Drawing the Colt and charging off after Vernon, Clint snarled, "I'll feel a whole lot better once I get my hands on that weasel."

TWENTY-NINE

With the sting of that first hit quickly fading, Clint was able to move faster through the bushes without worrying about breaking his leg in the process. Even though he was cursing Vernon under his breath the whole way, he had to hand it to the little jerk. He sure knew how to pick his spot to make this move.

Not only was there a thick tangle of bushes in this stretch of the trail, but the ground was uneven enough that Clint couldn't move at top speed. Instead, he was forced to jog while testing the ground with his boot and glancing around for logs, rocks or any number of things that could trip him up.

Fortunately, Vernon's steps were rushed and the chain was still dragging behind him noisily, like a leash dragging from the neck of a runaway dog. As much as Clint wanted to run ahead and pounce on the prisoner, he refrained from doing so.

"Aw, hell!" came Vernon's voice, followed by the heavy thump of something hitting the ground.

And that, Clint thought with a grin, was why a man shouldn't run on uneven ground.

"Son of a bitch! Don't come any closer," Vernon hollered.

Just as Clint took another step forward, something came speeding at his head. Clint was just able to duck out of the way as a rock sailed over him. As he crouched on one knee, he saw Tara moving up to him. Since he hadn't heard her alongside him this whole time, he motioned for her to swing around to one side while he moved ahead.

Tara acknowledged Clint's request with a nod and crept through the brush, as if she was too light to break a twig under her foot.

"Where do you think you're going, Vernon?" Clint asked loudly to give Tara a bit more cover. "You don't even have a gun."

There were the sounds of some more movement, but they weren't footsteps. Instead, it sounded more like a sack being rolled on the ground.

Vernon let out a grunt and then said, "I know this trail a hell of a lot better than the two of you!" More sounds, this time like something being dragged. "I can disappear into a hole and you'd never find me!"

Clint moved his way forward and saw Vernon lying in the dirt, grabbing a leg. Vernon spotted Clint immediately and he swung the chain toward him once more.

Still feeling the sting from the last time he'd caught that chain, Clint backed up a bit to let the heavy manacle thump into the dirt. Before Clint could reach out and grab the piece of filthy, bloody iron, it was pulled back to disappear into the bushes.

Vernon let out a few more grunts before letting out a steadier breath.

"Aw, hell," Clint grunted as he peeked ahead and saw the other man get back to his feet and sprint away.

Just as Clint took off after him, he quickly found the stump that was half buried in the ground. It must have been

that stump that had tripped Vernon up, and Clint's own re-
flexes were barely enough to allow him to hurdle the obsta-
cle before repeating Vernon's mistake.

Clint gritted his teeth and started running the moment
his boots touched down on the other side of that stump. Already, he could hear Vernon speeding through the bushes.
His instincts told him that the prisoner was gaining ground
on him and doing it fast.

Rather than study the ground in front of him, Clint did
his best to stay in Vernon's wake. If the prisoner did know
the lay of this land as well as he claimed, the tactic should
allow Clint to gain some ground. Either that, or Clint was
rushing headfirst into a few broken bones of his own.

With his legs churning against the ground, Clint focused
on the fleeting glimpses of Vernon that he managed to
catch. All he saw was the occasional boot, the glint of light
off a metal link, or a nervous face peering back at him
through rustling leaves.

As much as Clint wanted to take a shot at that nervous,
rat-like face, he kept reminding himself of Tara's plea to
keep him alive.

Alive or nothing.

Those words echoed through his brain, reminding him
that Vernon was either kept alive through this, or all of their
efforts so far would be for nothing.

Feeling his breaths starting to come in heavier gasps,
Clint knew that he wouldn't be able to keep up the chase at
full speed for much longer. And since shooting Vernon
right now was out of the question, he holstered the Colt and
fitted the strap in place to keep the gun from slipping out.

Now that both hands were free, Clint took a few more
bounding steps, while extending both arms in front of him.

Vernon was getting closer. The prisoner's own breaths
were rough and loud. Every other wheezing exhale was
punctuated by a curse. His steps were becoming more er-

ratic and the movement of his body was resembling a top
that was wobbling as it ran toward the end of its spin.

After stepping forward one more time, Clint planted his
feet and pushed off to launch himself toward Vernon. One
of Clint's hands closed on nothing but dusty air. The other
managed to snag hold of Vernon's boot.

"Gotcha," Clint said triumphantly.

Vernon was still trying to move forward, but was
stopped short when his foot was grabbed. He lost his mo-
mentum in a second and flopped face-first onto the ground.
Before the impact had a chance to register in his head, he
was already twisting around and swinging his other leg in a
kick aimed at Clint's face.

Clint pulled back as quickly as he could, but couldn't
avoid catching a piece of Vernon's heel on his chin. The
impact rattled him a bit, but wasn't enough to shake him
loose. Instead, Clint tightened his hold on the man and
even managed to pull him in a foot or two.

Having gotten this far, Vernon wasn't about to give up
now. While snapping his free leg out one more time, he
leaned toward Clint to smash his manacled wrist against
flesh and bone.

Those manacles pounded against Clint's shoulder,
barely missing his temple. With that pain still flooding
through him, Clint felt another blow land directly on top of
the first as Vernon rapped his manacles against him yet
again.

Grinning as he prepared to put Clint down for good,
Vernon suddenly found that his manacled hand wasn't able
to move. He hadn't seen Clint reach out to take hold of it,
but that's exactly what happened. And now that Clint had a
hold of Vernon's wrist, he was pulling him in.

While tugging Vernon's arm, Clint lashed out with a
straight punch. Even after the punch had landed, Clint kept
pulling until he thought he might knock Vernon's skull

clean off his shoulders. The impact was so satisfying to Clint that it was almost enough to wipe away the lingering pain from the blows that he'd been forced to take.

Of course, it wasn't enough to numb him to the kick that Vernon managed to sneak in under Clint's extended arm.

This time, Clint was the one surprised by Vernon's speed. Even though the little rodent was covered in dirt and blood, breathing like it was his last moment on earth, and flailing like a grounded fish, he still managed to keep going. The kick that landed against Clint's ribs had just enough of a bite to it to loosen his grip.

Vernon pulled his foot away, flopped around and scrambled to his feet. A wheezing laugh started to mix in with his labored breaths as he turned his back to Clint. His victory came up short, however, when he saw Tara lean forward from a nearby clump of bushes with her rifle against her shoulder.

"Fun's over, Vernon," she said.

THIRTY

"Give me your hand," Tara demanded.

Gazing down the wrong end of that rifle, Vernon didn't put up a fight. He extended his free arm and cowered in front of her.

"Not that one," she said. "The one with the iron hanging from it."

Reluctantly, Vernon complied.

Tara had seen Clint take enough punishment from those manacles for her to know better than to let that arm stay free. The moment her fingers closed around his wrist, however, she felt it immediately start to slip away.

Vernon's manacled hand was coated in just as much blood as the one he'd gotten free. That blood might as well have been grease, and it allowed him to pull it free while grabbing for Tara's rifle with his other hand.

"Fun's only started, lady," Vernon snarled.

Just as Vernon got ahold of the rifle, Clint stormed up behind him. Clint had gotten a loose hold on the back of Vernon's shirt when he saw the business end of Tara's rifle pointing straight at his face. Reflexively, Clint ducked and moved to one side. From that new vantage point, he could see how Tara was struggling to regain control of her weapon.

As Vernon jerked the rifle toward him, Tara's finger snapped against the trigger and the rifle barked loudly.

Even though the bullet whistled well over Clint's head, he didn't appreciate being there at all. He choked that down and reached for the section of the barrel between Tara's and Vernon's hands. With a quick twist and then a pull, Clint shoved the rifle against Vernon's thumb. This time, the blood covering Vernon's hands worked against him and the rifle came free of his grasp.

The moment he saw Tara regain her grip on the rifle, Clint swept one leg out to catch both of Vernon's knees. The prisoner's legs swept right out from under him, leaving a shocked look on his face as he started to fall straight to the ground.

With attacks coming from every angle, Vernon was too confused to decide what to do. Because of that, he broke his fall with his own jaw as his face smacked against the packed earth and the rest of his body crumpled into a heap.

Clint's eyes were still on the man, even though it looked impossible for Vernon to move a muscle. "Is he really down?" he asked.

"One way to be certain," Tara replied as she stepped forward to stand over her prisoner. Without so much as a blink, Tara upended her rifle so she could take hold of the barrel. From there, she sent the stock down onto Vernon's head where it landed with a solid crack.

Whatever fight might have been left in the prisoner didn't survive long after that. Vernon's limbs went limp and he let out a soft groan.

"Jesus," Clint said as he got to his feet and dusted himself off. "Things sure would be easier if we could just shoot this asshole."

"I didn't think you were the killing type," she replied with a smirk.

"Not generally, but this one's driving me to it."

"I won't tell if you won't."

"As tempting as that is, let's just make sure this doesn't happen again." Clint scooped Vernon up and slung him over his shoulder. "How about you cover me with that rifle? If he moves, don't worry about hitting me."

"Understood."

Clint carried Vernon back to where the horses were waiting. He felt like a hunter from the distant past, returning with that night's meal.

Vernon started to squirm a bit more as his face began to twitch.

Wriggling and sucking in a few breaths, he made a few grunting sounds, before finally snapping awake. When his eyes opened, he let out a surprised yelp.

"Holy shit!" he said as he saw the ground passing by only a few feet from his nose. "Where the hell am I?"

"On your way to Harbinger," Clint replied. "What did you think?"

"What the . . . where . . . how did . . . ?" Vernon stammered as he struggled to get a feel for what was going on.

All he could tell at the moment was that he couldn't move. Although it looked as if he was falling to the ground one more time, he hadn't hit the dirt just yet. Instead, his face just kept bouncing toward the earth and the breath was squeezed from his chest.

Clint reached back to check on Vernon. Since the prisoner was wrapped from his knees up to his shoulders in rope, and slung over Eclipse's back, Clint had only needed to look at him once or twice during the ride. Every time he caught sight of Vernon in that state, Clint couldn't help but smile.

"You know what he looks like?" Clint asked as he looked over to Tara. "A worm. He looks like a big ol' inchworm."

She laughed and took a look for herself. "I guess sometimes looks aren't deceiving."

"Yeah?" Vernon spat. "Well this ol' inchworm is gonna put the both of you in the ground before this is over. Mark my words."

Clint reached back to rap the back of his hand against Vernon's head. "Shut up before I do it the hard way."

Despite the mean look on Vernon's face, he kept his mouth shut and his comments to himself. He did his best to glare at Clint threateningly, but that was quite a chore, considering his situation.

"Don't worry, Vernon," Clint said cheerfully. "We're about to make camp and then tomorrow we'll be in Harbinger. If you still want to cooperate with us, I'll even let you have something besides fresh soil for dinner. What else could a growing inchworm want?"

Vernon rolled his eyes and let his head hang as close to the ground as it could. Even though he would never agree with Clint, he had to admit that he could feel the hook sinking awfully deep into his mouth.

THIRTY-ONE

Thanks to some help pulled from Vernon, they set up camp less than half a day's ride outside of Harbinger. Tara scouted ahead and confirmed that there was a town right where Vernon said it would be. Clint found a clearing that backed against a rock wall and was surrounded by thick bushes and trees on nearly every other side. As far as defensible campsites went, they didn't get much better than that.

It was just past sundown and the scent of baked beans and pork was still lingering in the air. In the next few moments, the scent of brewing coffee drifted up to join into the mix. Tara sat down and leaned in a little to pull some more of the scents into her nose.

"That smells great," she said. "You're one fine cook."

"It's not too hard," Clint replied. "Just stick to things that can't be messed up. Later on, I might scramble some eggs."

"I'll look forward to it."

After a bit of a pause, Tara settled herself against her bedroll with her legs curled beneath her. "I wanted to apologize for what happened."

"What happened?"

125

"You know . . ." Rather than say what she was thinking, she reached out to brush her fingers against Clint's bruised face. "Strictly speaking, he's my prisoner and you're the one that took all the punishment when he tried to get away."

"I'm the one who volunteered," Clint said. "I knew it wouldn't be easy." While using a stick to prod the embers of the campfire, Clint added, "Of course, I wasn't thinking it would be this hard either."

Although Tara smiled at that, her expression didn't last long. Soon, it was replaced by a thoughtful stare pointed into the flames beneath the coffeepot. "What are we going to do in Harbinger?"

"Anything we can."

"I know, but what does that mean? How much . . ." She trailed off as her attention shifted to Vernon. When she saw that Vernon was sound asleep, wrapped up like a pig in a blanket, she dropped her voice to a whisper and said, "How much can two of us do if this thing is half as big as he says it is?"

Clint didn't say a word. He stood up and started walking away from the crackling fire. After a few steps, he motioned for Tara to follow him.

On the other side of the bushes surrounding the campsite, a stream meandered its way toward the Green River. The stream was about ten paces wide and was shallow enough for the bright light of the moon to make it all the way down to its bottom.

At the spot where Clint and Tara stopped, the water was rushing over a cluster of small rocks. It wasn't exactly dangerous white water, but it made enough noise to keep their voices from carrying.

Clint dumped the coffee from his tin cup and bent down to scoop up some of the stream's water. It was so cool that he could feel it working its way throughout his whole body. "Our friend back there has told us more than enough for me to know that his ears are almost as big as his mouth. He doesn't need to hear every little thing that we say."

"Especially when I make it sound like we're relying on him," Tara said with a slow nod. "I should have known better than to talk like that when he could have been awake and listening."

"That's not a problem at all. I was more concerned about him hearing what I wanted to say to you."

"Really?" she asked as she looked up with a grin. "And what might that be?"

"That I don't have any clue what we're truly going up against in Harbinger. My gut tells me that Tucker sent us out on this job as a way to unofficially take a swing at whoever killed one of his men. But if we can believe a word that's come out of Vernon's mouth, any U.S. marshal who valued his career would have wanted to lead this charge himself."

"Either that or . . ." Tara trailed off so she could take a deep breath and face Clint once more. ". . . or Tucker is one of the crooked officials that Vernon was talking about."

"Yeah. There's that possibility too." Clint took a sip of water and savored the crisp flavor as it splashed down his throat. "But he could have set up a better trap than just trying to jump us on our way out of town. He also would have tried killing us again by now or at least tried to get ahold of Vernon before he started talking."

"There's no way for anyone to know everything that's going to happen, Clint. All of those things could be mistakes or just luck swinging one way or another."

"Anyone who makes their living at blackmail or by using crooked politicians is real good at thinking things through. They'd have to be, otherwise there would be no way for them to keep track of everything they've got cooking."

The expression on Tara's face was a mix of uncertainty and suspicion. When he saw that, Clint explained, "It's like trying to lie to dozens of different people. You need to spend a lot of time keeping track of what lies you've told and second-guessing anything anyone might say to trip you up."

"You sound like you know a lot about that," Tara said.

"Only because I've been forced into tripping up a lot of liars. Play high stakes poker more than once without losing everything you own and you'd become pretty good at that too."

"I never was too good at poker, but I grew up with some troublesome little brothers. I guess I picked up my nose for trouble that way."

"That would do the trick. What does that nose tell you about our friend Vernon?"

"That he's a slimy little toad who would stab us in the back the first chance he got," she replied without hesitation. "But I also think he would stab anyone in the back if it meant saving his own skin. That includes whoever he's working for."

"I agree. I also think he could be a real help in getting us into Harbinger and finding whoever is behind this whole thing. Once we get there, we'll find out how big it really is. If Vernon was exaggerating, we could do some real damage on our own."

"And what if he wasn't?"

"Then we get out and send for help. Someone like Tucker needs good reason to make his move. He's also smart enough to know that where corruption is concerned, it's awfully hard to find anyone you can trust. That's why he wanted us to do this."

Laughing, Tara said, "You're the mystery man and I'm the one that nobody's bothered to bribe?"

"Something like that."

Tara stepped forward until she was almost nose to nose with Clint. Keeping her eyes on him, she reached down to slowly take the cup from his hand. "You know something?" she asked after taking a drink and licking her lips.

"You're the first man who's been with me this long and not tried to get their hands on me."

"I'd be lying if I told you I wasn't thinking about it once or twice."

"Well, I'm thinking about it right now. Since we'll be heading into Harbinger tomorrow and might be heading straight into a powder keg, I'd like to take advantage of this night."

Clint tossed the cup and slipped his hands around Tara's waist. She pressed herself against him and started grinding her hips slowly.

"And what a night it is," Clint said.

THIRTY-TWO

Tara was light as a feather when Clint picked her up and carried her to a thick tree at the edge of the stream. She rested her hands on his shoulders and smiled expectantly as she was set down and Clint moved in close to her.

Her hat dropped off with a twitch of her head and she quickly tussled her hair into a wispy cascade of blonde waves. When she felt Clint's hands move up along her sides, she leaned back against the tree and arched her back while letting out a smooth, satisfied moan.

Clint kept his eyes locked on Tara's so he could examine their color and the flutter of her lashes. Those eyes were a light shade of blue, which had looked green more than once when Clint had seen them before. As he studied them, his hands continued their exploration of her body, tracing every subtle slope.

When his hands brushed along the sides of her pert breasts, Tara trembled slightly and let out another breath. This time, she whispered, "Yes, Clint," as she closed her eyes and writhed against the tree.

Although Clint allowed his fingertips to linger for a moment at the bare skin of her neck, he was too anxious to move them down again. Tara didn't seem to mind one bit as he retraced his steps and cupped her breasts in both hands. As he made small circles with his hands, he could feel her nipples growing hard against his palms.

She writhed some more. This time, her hips moved forward until she found his. Keeping her eyes closed, she put on a naughty smile when her leg brushed against the hardness in his crotch. She then moved that leg around to slide up and down Clint's thigh while grinding her own hips against his erection.

When he felt her moving between his legs, Clint went from unbuttoning her shirt to almost tearing it open. Fortunately, her buttons gave way with a bit of effort and only a few were lost in the process. Beneath her shirt, Tara wore a white cotton camisole that was trimmed with a thin row of lace.

The pale moonlight washed over her, accentuating the curves of her breasts as well as her rigid nipples. Clint slid his hands along her front before finding a hint of bare skin at her midsection. When he slipped his hands beneath the camisole, he could feel her tight stomach moving quickly to the increasing pace of her breaths.

"God, you're torturing me," she whispered as she quickly unbuckled his jeans.

Clint peeled off her shirt, leaving just the camisole. He also slid her jeans down, lowering himself to his knees in the process. When she stepped out of her pants, Clint was on his knees in front of her. From there, he reached out to grab her hips and pull her close so he could press his mouth against her warm little pussy.

Tara started to let out a surprised squeal, but it caught in her throat. Instead, she grabbed his hair and pulled him closer while draping one of her legs over Clint's shoulder. Looking down at him, she watched as he opened his mouth and licked the inside of her thigh. She needed to lean against the tree for support when she felt his tongue slip over her clit and then ease into her.

While Tara was still breathless, Clint began working his way up. He nibbled a line up her stomach and kissed his way between her breasts. When he got up to her ear, he could feel her hands working to pull down his pants so she could wrap her fingers around his rigid penis.

"I can't wait, Clint. I need you inside me."

As she said that, Tara guided his cock between her legs and fit it into her pussy. Clint pumped his hips forward a little bit at a time before finally sliding all the way inside of her. As he buried his cock in her, he let out the breath he'd been holding since he felt her warm lips enveloping him. Her body wrapped around him tightly and they stayed that way without moving for at least a minute or two.

Cupping her in both hands, Clint held on to Tara's tight little buttocks and started thrusting in earnest. Her eyes snapped open and fixed on him as he started thrusting between her legs. She opened her legs for him and arched her back while scraping her fingernails along the back of his shoulders.

After thrusting into her one more time, Clint felt Tara's hands pressing against his chest. With a mischievous grin on her face, she moved him back far enough so she could step away and walk toward the stream.

Clint watched her move toward the water. The moonlight accentuated the curve of her hips and the smooth lines of her body. Her hair drifted in the breeze as she turned to look at him over her shoulder and motion for him to follow with a slow curl of her finger.

More than happy to oblige, Clint walked up behind her as she lowered herself onto her knees and crawled to within inches of the water's edge. Her backside formed an inviting line as she pressed her chest against the soil and stretched her arms out to slip into the water.

Clint knelt down behind her and rubbed his hands along the small of her back. When Tara straightened up to lean back against him, he could feel her tight backside rubbing against his cock. Reaching around with both hands, Clint cupped her breasts, feeling the wet camisole cling to her like a second skin.

After twisting around to kiss him, Tara leaned forward again and arched her back. Clint placed his hands upon her hips and positioned himself. With a little shifting and the forward motion of his own body, he soon felt the tip of his cock sliding into her. From behind, he was able to pull her to him while driving into her even deeper than before. When he was finally in all the way, they both let out a contented sigh.

Tara was on all fours now. The ends of her hair brushed along the surface of the water as she rocked back and forth to the rhythm of Clint's thrusts. Her hands sank below the water and when Clint pounded into her with a little more force, she started making fists in the wet mud.

The breeze was cool as it washed over them. Clint looked up to see the glittering blanket of stars overhead. When he looked down again, he saw a heavenly body of another kind. Tara's back was smooth and perfectly textured as she wriggled back and forth.

Clint reached out to trace his fingers along the curve of her spine. When he got all the way up to her shoulder, he took hold of it and pumped all the way inside of her.

Tara responded by tossing her head back and bucking against him. The smile on her face could be seen as clear as day in the reflection upon the water.

Taking hold of her other shoulder as well, Clint started pumping into her harder, again and again. Clint had noticed Tara's tight little body more than once since they'd met. But even he was surprised by how finely toned and muscled she was. Every one of her curves was tight, while also being nicely rounded. Clint especially enjoyed the way her bottom shook when he slapped against it.

Soon, Tara reared up again until she was almost completely upright. Her backside kept just enough of its angle so Clint could continue to slide in and out of her. She reached over her shoulder and slid her fingers through Clint's hair as she started to let out little gasping breaths.

He could feel her pussy tightening around him. The way her body was pressed against his made the sensation of being inside her all the more intense. Soon, he was breathing heavily as well and could feel as both of their climaxes rushed in on them.

Wrapping his arms around her, Clint pumped into her one more time before exploding within her. Tara's entire body shook with a powerful orgasm until his arms were the only thing holding her up.

THIRTY-THREE

Harbinger appeared to be a sleepy, dirty little town hidden away in Utah. Of course, that could only be seen by those who actually got close enough to see the town. Those who were given permission to do so were able to ride in along a broken-down trail, which was marred by so many overlapping wagon ruts that the road was just shy of impassable.

Most everyone who found that road was able to use it without expecting anything more than the usual troubles associated with travel. One of the town's best assets was how unappealing it was to nearly every one of a person's five senses.

For those few who were deemed unwelcome, on the other hand, the trip was considerably more unpleasant.

When he'd first heard about it, Clint didn't believe what Vernon was telling him. He listened to the prisoner's entire explanation, waited until the man was finished talking and then said, "Bullshit."

"What?"

"You heard me. Am I supposed to believe that?" Clint shook his head and let out a disgusted breath. "If you were going to lie to me, I'd have thought you'd come up with something better than that."

135

"Honest!" Vernon whined. "I'm telling you the truth, so help me!"

"I won't be helping you out of those ropes, that's for damn sure. Not after hearing a story like that."

Vernon squirmed in his bindings, which were the same ones that he'd been wrapped in since the beginning of the day. The ropes themselves were the same ones he'd worn after his escape attempt and had the sweat stains and rancid odors to prove it. Even though he'd been allowed out of his bonds to eat and relieve himself, he didn't feel at all the better for it.

"Getting out of these damn ropes is all I can think of," Vernon said. "I'd hack off a toe if it meant riding like a human being again instead of some kind of . . . some kind of carpet."

Tara smirked as she looked down at him. It was late in the afternoon and they'd been riding since sunup. Harbinger was less than two miles away and they'd stopped to have a word with their prisoner before going any farther.

After dropping Vernon to the ground and propping him against a tree, Clint had seemed more than patient with the prisoner. He'd asked a few questions and Vernon had provided some answers. Now, the politeness had seemingly come to an end.

"You mean to tell me that there is some kind of death squad patrolling the perimeter of this town?" Clint asked.

Without blinking an eye, Vernon nodded.

"Then how come we haven't seen anyone on this trail all day long?"

Shrugging, Vernon said, "We're probably not close enough. I can't exactly get my bearings when I'm bouncing around on the back of that horse!"

Tara rode around Eclipse so she could look down at Vernon. "You know we can find out if you're lying easily enough?"

"Of course I do," Vernon replied. "I ain't stupid."

"Then why don't you just start by telling—"

"Jesus Christ," Clint interrupted.

Tara glanced over and found that Clint wasn't even looking at her or Vernon. Instead, he was staring through the crook of an old tree that marked the spot where they'd turned off the trail. "What is it?" she asked.

But Clint was already grabbing hold of the strands of rope, which he'd loosened enough to use as handles. "We need to get moving."

"What, Clint? What's wrong?"

After draping Vernon across Eclipse's back, Clint climbed into the saddle and flicked the reins. Tara managed to keep up with him as he steered the Darley Arabian around the opposite side of the tree. Once they were there, Clint pointed and asked, "Do you see them?"

At first, Tara saw nothing but trees and more trees. Then, after staring at the spot where Clint was pointing for a little while longer, she nodded. "Are they all headed this way?"

"Yep," Clint said as he took another look at the four riders charging toward them. "They sure are."

Clint had spotted the rifles in the men's hands right away. Of course, the riders weren't doing anything to hide the guns they carried. Indeed, they brandished their weapons as if they wanted any and everyone to see what was coming their way.

And just as soon as Clint steered Eclipse away from them, he spotted another couple of riflemen rounding a bend in the distance.

"How the hell did they know we were here?" Clint asked himself more than any of the others.

"They watch this trail for miles in every direction," Vernon said. "I told you that much just a few minutes ago."

"What are we supposed to do now that they're here?" Tara asked.

Vernon strained his neck to get a look at her. "You pray they decide to let you pass."

"Well," Clint said as he took hold of the reins and gave them a snap. "I didn't come this far just to turn back now."

"That's not a good idea," Vernon warned in a taunting voice.

But Clint had already steered Eclipse onto the trail and got moving toward Harbinger. The first traces of the town could be seen and they weren't much more than a few shacks clumped together. The way the riders closed ranks in front of Clint, one might have thought those shacks were the Promised Land.

Most of the riders were lined up about fifty yards in front of Clint and Tara. Some more of the riflemen came in on either side of the trail, leaving about twenty yards of space between them and their target.

"We just need to get into town," Clint said. "I'm taking a bounty in to be collected and we just need to water our horses. After that, we'll be moving along."

Clint's words were still echoing through the air when the first series of shots exploded from the rifles to kick up so much dirt on the trail around the horses' feet that the dust caught in all their throats.

"See?" Vernon said between hacking coughs. "I told you so."

THIRTY-FOUR

Tara's hand went for her rifle, but Clint spotted the motion and reached out for her.

"No," Clint ordered. "Don't pull that gun."

"But they're shooting at us!"

"And if they'd meant to do any harm, they would have been aiming for something other than the ground at our feet."

Glancing around at the riflemen, Tara saw that the riders were still sighting down their rifles, but not firing another round at them. At least, not just yet.

"They've already got the drop on us and outnumber us three to one," Clint said. "Let's just see what they want."

Reluctantly, Tara eased her hand away from her rifle. "All right. I just hope you know what you're talking about."

Clint shifted in his saddle to face the two riders that were approaching them. "So do I," he said under his breath. He reached behind his back to tap Vernon. "How do we get past these men?"

Vernon let out a few uncertain grunts and squirmed just enough to cause Eclipse to shift on his feet.

"Remember our deal?" Clint asked. "You help me and

139

I'll keep you alive rather than hand you over to the men that must want you dead a dozen times over."

"Yeah," Vernon grunted. "I remember."

A few of the riders had separated from the rest and were approaching Clint and Tara. They moved cautiously, staring daggers at them over the barrels of their rifles. All of the riders were dressed in dark clothes with brown bandannas around their necks. They might have looked like cowboys to those who didn't know any better, but to Clint they had the mannerisms of guns for hire.

"Then tell me what I need to know," Clint hissed. "And do it quick. If we don't make it through here, I won't have much need to tend to your well-being."

After letting out a disgruntled breath, Vernon said, "Tell them you're here to visit Harley's Antiques."

"Is that all?"

"Yeah. That should get you through."

"One last thing," Clint added before the riders got close enough to hear him. "Are these fellows going to recognize you?"

"I don't know. Maybe."

That was all Clint had time to say before the riders came to a stop less than five paces in front of him.

"What's your business here?" the lead rider asked.

Clint kept his hands in sight and an easy smile on his face. "I told you, I'm here to collect a bounty. Also, I'm here to do a little shopping. I hear Harley's Antiques has some real good prices."

For a moment, Clint didn't think the rider had a clue what he was talking about. The man stared back at him with a face chiseled from stone. He didn't even blink as the seconds ticked away like hours. Finally, his eyes shifted in their sockets so he could take another look at the unusual trio.

"Who's the bounty?" the rider asked.

"Just some horse thief," Clint replied.

Although he smirked at the way Vernon was trussed up and tossed across Eclipse's back, he didn't seem to care enough to take a closer look. He did, however, take a closer look at Tara. "What about her?"

"I'm his partner," Tara replied before Clint could say a thing. "And we were told that we could stop by here any time we wanted the last time we passed through. You got a problem, then take it up with Judge Murphy over in Billings. He likes to keep to his schedules and this is just holding us up."

Although the lead rifleman practically stared a hole through Tara's skull, she glared right back at him without a flinch. Finally, the rifleman steered his horse out of the trail and nodded toward town. "Go on."

That was all they needed to hear. Clint tipped his hat and flicked his reins. Tara gave the man a nod, but instantly regretted it when she got a leering smile in return. Vernon just lay across Eclipse's back like an oversized bedroll.

Before they even crossed into Harbinger, the riflemen had all disappeared.

"See?" Vernon grunted.

"Shut it," Tara said sharply.

THIRTY-FIVE

As they rode down the main streets of Harbinger, Clint and Tara looked around to take in what little sights there were. After just a few glances in either direction, both of them had unappreciative looks on their faces.

"What a hole," Tara said.

Clint nodded. "Yeah. I've seen better, myself. By the way, who's Judge Murphy?"

"He's a real judge. He's also not known for being the straightest arrow of them all."

"Is he on Zack Richards's payroll?"

"Could be. I just thought that those guards would have a notion about the dirty dealings of their boss and that if I dropped an official's name, it would make us seem more like we belonged here."

Hearing that gave Clint a bit of a knot in his stomach. He wasn't exactly opposed to taking risks, but he preferred to keep from betting his life on them.

"Quick thinking," he said. "Next time warn me before you think so quickly."

She laughed. "I will. Where to now?"

"Well, apart from being a sty, this place seems to be like plenty of other towns."

"Have you picked out your favorite restaurant yet?"

"So far, I think we'd be better off cooking for ourselves. There's a room for rent over there," he said, pointing to a short row of houses at the end of the block. "Let's give the horses a rest, catch our breath and take it from there."

"Finally," Vernon groaned. "If I don't get out of these ropes, I'll be forced to make a mess."

"Make all the mess you want," Clint replied. "You're wrapped up tight enough to keep the stink down to a minimum. At least, the stink shouldn't be bad for us."

By this time, Vernon knew to keep his mouth shut and wait a bit longer. That tactic paid off because in half an hour, they were getting themselves situated in a good-sized room with pictures of strangers hanging from every wall. Apart from the clutter, it was a whole lot better than many hotel rooms Clint had seen.

Vernon let out a grateful sigh as the ropes loosened and came off, one coil at a time. Once he was free, he was too busy working the kinks from his arms and legs to worry about trying another escape.

"Where's Zack Richards?" Clint asked.

Vernon rubbed his knee, found an itch and then started scratching it like a dog with a tick under its fur. "How the hell should I know? I haven't left your sight since we got here."

"When was the last time you saw him? Where would you go to find him if it was just you here?"

Too tired to fight with Clint anymore, Vernon found another itch on his nose and busied himself with that. "Try the Number Four Saloon."

"Where's that?"

"Right between the Number Three and Five."

Clint's expression didn't change in the slightest. Instead, he kept his eyes focused upon Vernon until the prisoner let out a nervous grunt of a laugh.

"You got no sense of humor, Adams." Shifting his fin-

gers to the back of his neck, Vernon said, "It's two blocks
over at the end of Johnson Avenue. There ain't any street
signs, so just look for the biggest mess of horses tied up in
one place. You won't be far off the mark. You might want
me to go with you, though."

"Why's that?"

"You know those gunmen that met you outside of town?
Well, those are choirboys compared to the ones that Zack
surrounds himself with. If you go strutting into the Number
Four without a proper invitation, you'll get to know those
boys real well. Even some men that Zack's expecting get
roughed up if they come in uninvited."

"Do you know where Richards lives?"

Vernon thought about that for a few moments before
shaking his head. "I just met him at the Number Four. It's
not like I ever got invited for supper, you know. Speaking
of that, I haven't had much of anything to eat for a while."

"I can't promise a steak, but I'll scrounge up something
for you."

By the look on Vernon's face, he'd been expecting to
fight for his food. When he didn't get one, he looked plenty
relieved. "Appreciate it."

Before Clint could get too sentimental, there was a
knock on the door that was so fast and so powerful that it
rattled the wood against its frame. His eyes fixed upon Vernon suspiciously, but saw that the prisoner was more star-
tled than anyone else by the sudden noise.

"Can you see who's out there?" Clint asked.

Tara was already standing at the door. Shrugging, she
whispered, "There's no hole for me to look through."

"Then we'll just have to do this the old-fashioned way."
Even before Clint had finished saying that, another series
of heavy thumps echoed throughout the room. "Keep an
eye on him. I'll see who it is."

Tara drew her pistol and held it on Vernon while she
moved to the back of the room.

Although Clint didn't draw his modified Colt, he kept his hand on the grip and was ready to skin it at less than a moment's notice. He approached the door with steps that were so light, they didn't even make the floorboards squeak.

Ready for anything, Clint gripped the handle and pulled the door open a crack.

"You want me to be seen by the whole damn town?" Ed grunted when he saw a sliver of Clint's face. "Let us in!"

THIRTY-SIX

Clint pulled the door open a bit more and took a look outside. Sure enough, Ed and John were standing in the hallway. Both of the guards were anxious enough to jump out of their boots. Unwilling to wait another second, Ed reached out to push the door open. Clint was barely quick enough to jump aside in time.

"What are you two doing here?" Clint asked.

John walked into the room and closed the door most of the way. He stood there and gazed through the narrow opening for a while before fully closing the door. "We were just about to ask you that question," he said.

"I'm here because Marshal Tucker asked me to be here," Clint replied. "So is she."

Ed and John exchanged confused glances.

"We haven't seen you since you left without telling anyone where you were headed," John said.

"I know you two didn't know where I was going, but that was the idea." Very quickly, Clint gave the two men a brief account of what had happened since the last time he'd seen them. He finished his story with, "And then the two of you came knocking on my door."

"This is the fella you tracked down from that ambush?"

Ed asked as he stepped up to within a foot or two of where Vernon was sitting.

Clint nodded. "That's him."

For the first time since Clint had met Ed, the stocky guard grinned from ear to ear. It was anything but a happy expression. On the contrary, he looked at Vernon in much the same way that Vernon had eyed the last steak he'd been given.

"Remember me, asshole?" Ed asked. "I'm the man you and your friends tried to kill once Clint scared you off."

"What?" Clint asked. But he didn't need another word of verification. The look on Vernon's face told him more than enough.

"I . . . uhhh . . . I don't know what you mean," Vernon stammered.

But Ed would have none of it. In fact, now that John had gotten a chance to get a look at the prisoner, he stood at Ed's side wearing a similarly lethal expression.

"That is him," John said. "That son of a bitch tried to shoot me in the back."

"Sounds like the Vernon we've come to know and love," Tara said as she stepped up to stand next to Clint. She stuck out her hand and said, "I'm Marshal Locke."

Both of the guards snapped their eyes over to look at her.

"You're Marshal Locke?" John asked.

She nodded, obviously perplexed by the reaction she'd gotten. "Have we met?"

"Not as such, but we were told to look for you once we got here."

"Told by who?"

"Marshal Tucker."

Tara smiled and looked over to Clint. "See? I told you Tucker had something more up his sleeve."

"Well, here she is," Clint said. "Here I am. Here we all are. Now, what are you supposed to do?"

John broke into a tired smile. "We're here to put an end

to the same problem we started in on. Tucker sent us off and told us there would be others riding this way to divert anyone who might be watching for unwanted visitors."

"If we would've known you were the decoy," Ed said, "we wouldn't have been so quick to leave you behind."

"Always glad to be a help," Clint replied. To Tara, he said, "Remind me to have a word with Tucker once this is through."

Crossing her arms sternly, she replied, "You'll just have to follow me."

"Don't get too upset at the man, Clint," John said. "He was right in thinking that there were men watching for us to leave. All Tucker did was send out more than one to split the trail. It worked pretty good, considering we both got here intact."

"How did you two get here?"

"Like bats out of hell," Ed replied. "I never rode so hard as we've been doing since we left. We started off at a run after fighting off that first ambush and we ain't stopped running since. That's the only way we blew past them other ambushes."

"Other ambushes?" Clint asked.

"Yeah. I don't figure your ride was too leisurely."

Compared to what John and Ed were saying, that was the very word Clint would have used to describe his ride. In fact, it was seeming more and more like it wasn't he and Tara who were the bait after all.

"So you were supposed to look for me," Tara said. "What were you supposed to do next?"

"I seriously don't think Tucker knew much more than what he told us," John said. "All he told us was that the source of the trouble was in Harbinger. We were just told to sniff it out, see what we could do about it and send for re-inforcements once the time was right."

"I say that time is about five minutes after we make sure whoever is at the root of this is really here," Ed said. "After that," he added, while shifting his eyes back to Vernon, "we take care of this nasty little loose end."

"Not so fast," Clint said as he stepped in front of Vernon. "This loose end has a job to do. He's a witness."

"And do you really think he's gonna testify?" Ed asked. "If you trust him so much, why was he brought in here hog-tied like that?"

"I said he's a witness. I didn't say he was cooperative. Besides, Vernon here's proven he can be a help. Between him and Tara, we got here a whole lot easier than you two."

"All right then," Ed snarled. "Since you're the man with the witness and all the big plans, why don't you come up with what we should do."

"Actually," Clint said while looking down at Vernon, "I think we've got a pretty good idea."

THIRTY-SEVEN

The Number Four saloon was as easy to find as Vernon said
it would be. By the time the sun had dipped below the hori-
zon, the only street that was lit worth a damn was the one
holding all the sporting places. Every one of the deadly sins
was represented on that street. For a price, there were even
a few people who were more than happy to suggest a few
new ones.

Tara and Ed were the first ones to make their appearance. They walked arm in arm into the Number Four and
sat down at one of the many small tables. Actually, calling
what they had in front of them a table was being generous.
Apart from a few bigger ones in the back, most of the tables were hardly more than tall stools balancing on one leg.

Since the saloon was full of couples, Tara and Ed fit in
well enough. Then again, Ed was one of the only men in
the place who wasn't paying his companion for her time.

"I guess this is as good a spot as any," Ed said.

Tara looked around and then looked down at herself.
Rather than her normal riding clothes, she wore a light-
pink dress that cinched in tight around her middle. The
neckline dropped down just low enough to display the

rounded tops of her breasts, which practically spilled out altogether.

"I feel like an idiot in this thing," she said, while making yet another adjustment to the dress.

Doing his best not to let his eyes linger on her for too long, Ed replied, "But you fit in perfectly with the rest of the girls in here."

"I'm just glad I didn't have to pay much for it. I think the only reason that shop was still open was because it only caters to whores."

"That, and because there was an opium den in the back."

"What?"

Grinning, Ed looked over at her. "You couldn't smell it?"

Since she couldn't come up with a good answer, Tara simply plastered on a smile and waved for some drinks.

Ed was still laughing under his breath when the server came over to see what they wanted. Not too surprisingly, the server was wearing a dress fairly similar to Tara's.

"How long have they been in there?" John asked.

Clint was standing right next to the guard. Both of them leaned against the front of a saloon across the street and down a little ways from the Number Four. From that spot, they could see everyone walking in and out of the same door that Tara and Ed had used not too long ago.

"It's been about twenty minutes," Clint replied. "More or less."

"Think we should head in there?"

"That's not the plan. We're supposed to wait out here for at least an hour or until we see one of them signal to us."

"Or if we hear trouble," John reminded him.

"That's right, but we haven't heard either of those things and it hasn't been an hour, so just relax."

"I haven't taken an easy breath since I saw that kid laying dead on the ground. Senator Gray is a good man and Lord only knows how many other good men are targets of this maniac. If any of this gets out, there won't be a politician around who won't at least think about doing what this Richards fellow wants."

"Not every politician is crooked. I've met at least one or two that weren't bad."

"Yeah, but there's enough that are on the fence or on the wrong side of it to tip the balance. I also don't like sending that lady into that hornet's nest."

"She's a U.S. marshal," Clint said.

"Not a full marshal. That badge of hers makes her sort of a federal deputy."

"Either way, she knows what she's doing. I can vouch for that."

"Maybe, but—"

John was cut off by a sudden rush of movement coming from the Number Four. The front doors to the place flew open and a parade of men in black suits charged outside like a stampede. Most of the men wore holsters around their waists, but one of them in particular wasn't armed. He was the oldest of the bunch and was also the most visibly upset.

". . . any more of this," was what Clint could hear from his spot. As the men crossed the street, it became easier to hear what the man was saying.

"I've had it. He's gone too far! I don't care what happens, I'm through with this madness!"

The doors swung open again. Another group of men came storming out, but these already had their guns drawn. "You're not going anywhere," the lead gunman said.

John glanced over to Clint and asked, "You think that qualifies as trouble?"

THIRTY-EIGHT

Despite more than a few nervous glances over their shoulders, the men in the black suits kept moving down the street. The gunmen who'd stormed out of the Number Four after them kept right on their tails.

"No need to leave in a huff, Senator Grinbee," the lead gunman said.

Turning on his heels, the older man in the black suit shot a glare back at the others. "I can go wherever I please! I'm leaving this damn town and never coming back!"

"Fine. Zack would just like to conclude his businesses with you."

"It is concluded. Good night." With that, the senator and his men continued their quick pace down the street.

Although a few of the gunmen started after the senator, they were stopped by an outstretched hand from their leader. No explanation was given and none of the gunmen seemed to expect one. After the senator's group had made their way to the corner, the lead gunman nodded and took his restraining arm back.

Once that signal was given, all of the gunmen took off like a pack of wolves on the prowl.

• • •

"Are we really leaving town?" one of the senator's men asked.

Grinbee didn't break stride. In fact, he sped up, now that he could see his hotel in the distance. "You're damn right we're leaving. I've dealt with that animal for too long. It ends tonight."

"But I don't think that'll stop Rich—" The man who'd been keeping pace beside Grinbee was stopped in his tracks as a pistol butt swung out from a shadow and connected with his skull.

The rest of the men in the suits stopped and took a quick look at who'd knocked their partner unconscious. That slight pause was all the time that the gunmen needed before they swarmed out like cockroaches from the darkness.

"Ain't nobody walks out on Zack Richards," the leader of the gunmen said with a grin.

"We can talk about this," Grinbee said in a rush.

"Time for that's gone. You're not worth the trouble no more." Turning to face the man who'd crept in the closest to Grinbee's men, he nodded and said, "Kill them all."

Before any of the men in the suits could say a word, they were surrounded by hot lead that filled the air. Gunshots echoed loudly in the cramped quarters of the small, empty lot where the two groups had met up. Although a few of the suits had pulled their guns, not many of them actually got a shot off. Those few who did were too rushed to hit much of anything.

After those first shots were exchanged, the gunmen moved in closer to finish their job with a more personal touch.

The sound of knuckles cracking against jawbone drifted through the air. Only, the sound wasn't caused by Grinbee's men or any of their attackers. Instead, it came from Clint's knuckles slamming into the closest gunman he could reach.

Before any of the gunmen could see what was happening, John reached out from the shadow where he'd been hiding and grabbed the gunman that had moved directly in front of him. John's arm snaked around the gunman's throat and pulled him into the shadows. After that, there came a few loud punches, followed by a pained exhale.

"Who the hell are you?" the gunmen's leader snarled.

Clint stepped out from the alley he'd used to creep up on the gunmen and let his hand drift toward his Colt. "I'm the one that's telling you to clear out of here. You're surrounded."

"Bullshit." Without exchanging another word with Clint, the head gunman signaled to the others and raised his pistol.

John rushed forward quicker than a man his size had a right to move. In the blink of an eye, he disarmed the gunman closest to him and delivered a solid punch into the man's gut.

By this time, Clint had had enough time to survey the situation and size up his odds. There were six gunmen in all and two of them had already been knocked out. As he rushed forward to drive his knee into another gunman's stomach, Clint saw John drop another one of the men closer to him.

Once Clint's knee landed, the gunman forgot about his pistol and emptied his lungs in one gust. As he did that, he crumpled over and folded around Clint's knee. That made it even easier for Clint to bring his other knee up to slam into the gunman's face. With that brutal crunch echoing through the air, the gunman sputtered and collapsed.

The leader of the gunmen glanced around at what was left of his men. Apart from himself, there was only one other that was still standing. Even that one didn't seem to be as anxious for a fight as he'd been a few moments ago.

"Who are you?" the gunman snarled.

Clint took another look at the scene and found that the roles from a few seconds ago had been completely reversed. Now, it was the men in the black suits who were swarming over the gunmen. There were only a couple of the suits left, but they managed to relieve most of the gunmen of their weapons.

The only one who was left was the leader. He'd removed the second gun from his double-rig holster and was now inches away from aiming at Clint. "This don't change anything," he said. "Judge Richards is too powerful to be stopped like this."

"Judge Richards?" Clint asked. When he glanced over to John, he only got a confused shrug from the guard.

"We don't need this piece of shit anymore," the gunman said as he nodded toward Grinbee. "And it'll take a hell of a lot more than the two of you to do a damn thing about it." With that, the gunman snapped his arm up and took aim.

Clint managed to lift his modified Colt and pull the trigger.

Before the sound of his shot registered in the gunman's ears, he was already dropping to the earth. Before he hit the ground, he was dead.

"Oh my God," Grinbee said as his knees buckled and he dropped to the ground. "I think I'm going to be sick."

"No time for that, Senator," John said as he stepped forward to offer the politician a hand. "We need to get you out of here."

Grinbee squinted up at him and said, "John? Is that you?"

"Yes, sir."

Trembling with relief, Grinbee reached up and grabbed onto both of John's arms. Even then, he had a hard time climbing back onto his feet. "You don't know how happy I am to see you! I tried to bring in my own men, but they weren't allowed into town. Richards said he sent them home, but nobody's heard from them. I hired these boys to guard me while I'm here."

"They did a fine job," Clint said, without doing much to hide his sarcasm. "What brings you to Harbinger?"

"I . . . well . . . was trying to . . . I mean, I was—"

"Save it," John interrupted. "We know what's going on here and the only way for you to get out is to tell everything you know to a federal judge."

"Speaking of judges," Clint said, "I didn't know the man in the middle of all this was a judge."

"Then allow me to enlighten you on the most recent events," Grinbee said. "But please, let's do that somewhere else."

THIRTY-NINE

Senator Grinbee was a bundle of nerves every moment that he was still in sight of the gunmen. Even though their leader was dead, Grinbee still looked down at the body as if he expected it to get up and lunge for him. Although he settled down a bit when Clint and John escorted him away, Grinbee was doubly nervous when he saw where they were going.

"Are you insane?" Grinbee asked. "I just came from that damn saloon and you want me to go back?"

"Not inside," Clint assured him. "I need to be able to see that door."

"I don't care. After all I went through to get out of there, I'm not about to go back."

John looked the senator in the eyes and asked, "Do you really think you'll be safe anywhere in this town? Or do you think you can get past the men circling it on horseback?"

As much as Grinbee wanted to dispute what John said, he simply didn't have it in him. Letting out a breath that sounded like his last one on earth, he said, "Fine. What about those men I hired? Do you think they'll report to Richards since you sent them away?"

Clint shook his head. "After nearly getting killed tonight, those men don't need to be told to find someplace to hide and stay there until this blows over. Now, how about you tell us about this judge business?"

Grinbee blinked quickly a few times and sucked in a deep breath. "That man's crazy. He's blackmailed politicians across this country to get everything from small favors ranging up to setting his hired killers free hours after they land in jail somewhere.

"He got to me through my gambling. I was too ashamed to say anything about it before, but after everything that's happened since then, what I did seems like nothing."

"You ran up a debt with Zack Richards?" Clint asked.

"Not with him," Grinbee replied. "But Richards found out about it. I don't know how, but he found out all the same. He arranged to have my debts paid and even loaned me some money to keep me gambling for months after that." Hanging his head, Grinbee added, "Once I didn't have to account for any of my spendings, it got so easy to keep betting. Anyway, when it came time to pay up, I owed more than I could pay. That's when he started asking for favors."

"What kind of favors?"

"He asked me to arrange for a state grant to fall through on some land in my jurisdiction so he could sweep in and buy it up. Things like that which really didn't do any harm. Then he asked me what kinds of policies I was debating or what was going through the Congress. He started asking me to vote a certain way on some things and it turned out I wasn't the only one."

"Are you saying he's influencing events in Washington?" John asked.

"To a certain extent. That was all just a trial run, though. I think he wanted to see if he could do anything like that at all. When he found out he could, he started planning for more."

Clint was trying to keep his eyes on the door to the

Number Four as well as the senator. "Are you sure about this?"

Grinbee nodded. "The man's crazy. He thinks he can become richer and more powerful than anyone in the country by pulling strings and calling in favors like this."

"If he's got enough of the right people on his payroll," John said, "he could be right."

"Take it from me, gentlemen," Grinbee continued. "Plenty of what passes for official decisions is affected by someone owing someone else a favor. Sometimes, things like that can even survive a jury. Don't ask me how, but I've seen some downright travesties take place just because two crooked politicians shook hands."

Hearing that, both Clint and John turned their eyes to Grinbee. The senator felt both of their gazes and immediately started to squirm. "I've committed my sins," the senator said. "But I draw the line at bowing down to that rabid animal. He's gone too far and I couldn't look myself in the mirror if I did half the things he's asking."

"Like what?" Clint asked.

After taking a deep breath, Grinbee took one more look toward the Number Four. He reacted as if he was staring at an open grave. "Somehow, Richards got himself made into a judge. It can't be official, but he claims he's fit to walk into a court and bang a gavel.

"Now that he's done that much, he intends on selling his influence as a service to anyone with enough money to pay him. He asked me to sign on as some sort of second government that answers to him. All my years of struggling to get where I am, all the work I've done, all the sacrifices I've made will wind up being used to serve that crazy murderer!"

Leaning in to John, Grinbee whispered, "He's already started killing off the politicians who've turned him down. He's even had Senator Gray killed just so he could frame me for it. I'm telling you, this man is out of his mind."

When Clint looked back at the Number Four, he barely even saw the saloon itself. Instead, he was putting together everything he'd heard and seen since the first shot was fired at that Governor's Ball. What chilled him the most was the fact that, in that context, many of Grinbee's claims didn't seem so far-fetched.

"There's no way for Richards to do all of that," John pointed out. "It's impossible."

Keeping his eyes on the saloon, Clint replied, "Maybe, but Grinbee's right. Even if a fraction of those things get carried out, it's more than we can allow. This has already gone too far."

"That's not the end of it either," Grinbee said.

Clint looked over to the senator and found the older man to be shifting back and forth as if he was under the devil's stare. "So, let's hear the rest."

"If Richards doesn't get his way, he's going to start picking off the most uncooperative of the men on his pay-roll and he doesn't care how high up they are. Having these last few senators and judges shot was only the beginning."

"What good would that do?" John asked.

Grinbee merely shrugged and shook his head. "Don't ask me. I told you the man was crazy."

"Does he really have the connections to pull off a stunt like that?"

"I would have said no a while ago, but lately I'm not so sure. He's been able to reach out and do some terrible things after sending one or two telegrams to his men."

Letting out a troubled breath, Clint said, "That means the ones he'll want to kill right away are the men we'll most want to save. Even if he just gets a few of his targets, that tips the balance more in the wrong direction."

"What can we do against this, Clint? There's only the four of us and this thing spreads throughout the whole country. That is, if we can believe what we're hearing."

"We don't need to believe all of it. There's one major thing working in our favor."

"What's that?"

"No matter how big the body is, it's only got one head."

FORTY

An hour passed.

Two hours passed.

In that time, Clint had yet to see a sign from Tara or Ed. Neither of them had come out of the saloon and there hadn't been any more gunmen emerging from there. The only familiar face to come out of the saloon was John and he didn't look too happy.

"Are they still there?" Clint asked.

Once John got across the street to where Clint was waiting, he shrugged. "They were in there and they didn't seem to be in any trouble."

"Did they see you walk in?"

"Yep. Tara still didn't look happy about wearing that dress, but they didn't stand out from all the others in there. With all the noise in that place, I doubt they even heard the ruckus when Senator Grinbee left."

"Then why haven't they come out to check in, like we planned?"

"Probably because they'd managed to get themselves within spitting distance of Zack Richards himself."

"You know that for certain?"

John nodded. "I didn't get up close enough to talk to

them, but Tara pointed out a table that was more heavily guarded than an army payroll. Seemed to me like that was the man we're after."

"Did it look like they were in trouble?"

"No. They weren't even the only ones close to Richards. Seems like everyone in this town knows what's going on and looks at Richards like he's just a part of the scenery. Maybe that's why he thinks he can just roll out and toss orders to the rest of the world."

"I don't care for the reasons," Clint replied. "I don't even care if half of what Grinbee said is true. All I know for certain is that maniac gave the order to kill a United States senator and succeeded in having a young man killed just for doing his job. That's more than enough reason for me to go on."

"I'm with you."

"Then let's cut the chatter and get on with it."

Having spent so much time trying not to be seen, Clint felt like he was waving a torch to draw attention to himself as he crossed the street and headed for the Number Four Saloon. John walked right beside him. Both men kept their eyes forward and their hands hanging close to their guns.

Before they entered the saloon, Clint asked, "You ready?"

"As ready as I can be."

Nodding, Clint pushed open the door and started walking inside.

"That's them!" came a voice that grated all too familiarly against Clint's nerves.

Turning on the balls of his feet toward the sound of the voice, Clint spotted the very person he hoped he wouldn't see. "Vernon?"

It was Vernon, all right, and he wasn't alone. The weasel with the sunken cheeks and brushy goatee walked in an awkward stumble after having been off his feet for so long, but his anxiousness to move more than made up for it. He wore a triumphant smile on his face as he stabbed his finger repeatedly in Clint and John's direction.

"Right there!" Vernon said. "Them's the ones that took me!"

There were half a dozen others with Vernon. Most of them carried shotguns, but a few had their pistols drawn. While they were obviously not the same men who'd come after Senator Grinbee, these men had the same cruel glint in their eyes as they swept forward to surround Clint and John.

Although his instincts cried out for him to draw his modified Colt, Clint knew when he was beaten. For the moment, that's exactly what he was. There was no doubt in his mind that making any move at that moment could be fatal.

Vernon made certain to stay behind the other men. He kept his hands busy by rubbing at his arms and legs to try and get the blood flowing through them once more.

"No," Clint said to John when he saw the guard start to draw his weapon. "Don't give them a reason to pull their triggers."

John let out a slow breath and reluctantly moved his hand away from his holster. Raising his arms, he said to Clint, "Seems to me like these boys don't need much of a reason."

FORTY-ONE

Clint and John were taken into the Number Four, but not through the door they'd intended. Instead, they were led around to a side entrance that opened into a narrow kitchen with air thicker and hotter than a swamp. It stank of burnt food and moldy vegetables. The floor was almost totally covered by a carpet of bugs and rodents.

"If you're offered anything to eat," Clint said to John, "be sure to turn it away."

As John laughed under his breath, both of them felt gun barrels jab them in the small of their backs to keep them moving. Those could very well have been their own gun barrels, since their weapons had been taken from them the moment Vernon's reinforcements had gotten within arm's reach.

Once they were out of the kitchen, Clint and John were shoved down a narrow hallway at the edge of the saloon's main room. For a split second, they could see out to the crowded bar and tables. Once that split second had passed, however, they were shoved right back into another putrid room.

This time, it was a large storage area that was about the size of a small set of stables. Clint and John were herded to the back of that room and placed against the wall. From there, the armed escort stepped back and waited. Their weapons never once turned away from their targets.

"So how'd you manage to wriggle out of those ropes, Vernon?" Clint asked.

John locked eyes with the former prisoner and said, "Easy. It was probably time for him to shed his skin."

Vernon put on an ugly smile and made a noise that was something close to laughter. "Very funny, assholes. Who's the one at the wrong end of the gun, now? Think about that the next time you want to flap yer gums."

Shifting his eyes as though Vernon had left the room, Clint looked to one of the armed men in front of the line. Now that he'd gotten a chance to look over these men a bit more carefully, he could see some differences between them and the ones who'd attacked Grinbee. Namely, there were a few of them who didn't seem to belong.

"You weren't with the original bunch outside," Clint said to a man wearing a black suit. "Did you follow us in from a card game?"

The man had a dark complexion and a face that might have been carved from granite. His mouth was a thin, straight line that barely seemed capable of opening. He held his revolver in a steady hand, keeping it pointed directly at Clint.

The door that they'd just used came open again and two men stepped inside. One of them was a tall, slender figure and the other was dressed in a black suit similar to the one on the stone-faced gunman.

After looking Clint and John over for no more than a second or two, the taller man said, "Take them to Grinbee's hotel."

"All right, Mister Richards," replied one of the gunmen.

The rock-faced man in the black suit didn't move a muscle until he got a nod from the man in the suit next to Richards. After that, he lent a hand in herding Clint and John toward the room's second door.

"You're Zack Richards?" Clint asked as he moved along.

"That's right. Sorry we couldn't get better acquainted, but I've got some business to tend to."

"Maybe I could have a word with you after that."

"I don't think so. You'll be dead by then."

"That might not be a good idea."

"Really? And why's that?"

"Because the men who sent us already know where we are," Clint replied. "And if we don't check in, they'll send so many U.S. marshals into this place that they'll outnumber the rats you've got in the kitchen."

Zack didn't say anything, but he was obviously thinking about what he'd heard since he'd signaled for the hired guns to wait before leaving. Walking around to get in front of Clint and John, he studied their faces and then nodded to his men.

"Keep an eye on them," the man next to Richards said. "Nothing more for now. We'll come by as soon as possible."

"Are we still headed for the hotel, Mister Beakman?" the stone-faced gunman asked.

"Yes, Evander. That's where we'll want them to be found when the time comes. Nobody will question Grinbee's death once he's connected to the murder of these two, as well as Gray's assassination."

Suddenly, Zack's eyes narrowed and focused upon another man in the group. "Is that you, Vernon?"

Vernon nodded and smiled proudly. "Yes, sir, Mister Richards. The boys found me after I called for help from where these two had me tied up."

Responding to the look from Zack, one of the gunmen shrugged and said, "He was screaming so loud that the owner of the boardinghouse went to have a look. She thought there was a little girl being held prisoner, but found him instead. Vernon dropped our names, so we went to pick him up."

"Where's the rest of the men I sent with you?" Zack asked.

Vernon shook his head gravely. "They didn't make it. I just barely got away."

"Ran away is more like it," John snarled. "He ran squealing like a pig once the shots started going off and it was all we could do to catch up to him."

Judging by the unsettling look on Zack's face, he did not like what he was hearing.

"Who you gonna believe?" Vernon whined when he saw Zack's expression. "Them or me?"

Without much hesitation, Zack said, "Take him along with them other two. I don't have the stomach for cowards."

Vernon's eyes grew wide as saucers. "What!?"

But Zack had already turned and walked off. The hired guns took that as their cue to shove Clint, John and Vernon through the door.

FORTY-TWO

The streets of Harbinger had cleared out. It seemed as though everyone there knew when Zack's men were approaching, even if they weren't on his payroll. Like rats abandoning a sinking ship, they found somewhere safer to be and got there in a hurry.

As odd as the silence felt, Clint was glad for it. He could hear the steps of all the men behind him, as well as the two on either side. That way, he was able to get a sense of where everyone was and how far away they might be. Every little bit of knowledge was important when it came to making a move that might be his last.

Looking over to John, Clint saw the guard was thinking along those same lines. John returned Clint's look with a confirming nod, silently letting him know that he was ready.

Ready for what?

Clint was going to have to make that up as he went.

Just as Clint had pulled in a deep breath to steel himself, he heard the doors to the saloon fly open behind him. That was followed by the thump of feet against the boardwalk and the scrambling of a few of Richards's men as they turned to get a look.

"Get back inside!" one of the hired guns shouted.

The only response he got was in the form of a gunshot blasting through the unnaturally still air.

After that first shot, there was too much chaos for Clint to make any sense of it through sound alone. He kept his head low as he turned on his heels to get a look behind him. John followed suit and swung around to see Vernon dive for cover.

Standing in front of the saloon, Tara and Ed unleashed a hailstorm of lead at the guards. Even though Tara only had a Derringer in each hand, she was making her shots count and had already dropped one of the gunmen.

Ed gritted his teeth and took aim. He held his ground, even as the gunmen began firing off shots of their own.

While most of the guards were occupied with Tara and Ed, a few of them stayed close to Clint and John. Evander was one of those and the gunman in the black suit glared at Clint as if he was the one that had just shot at him.

Clint knew the distraction wouldn't last forever, so he balled up his fists and charged toward Evander. That sudden movement had its desired effect and took Evander by surprise. Clint was able to land a few punches to the man's stomach, which was just enough for him to realize that Evander's frame was covered with a thick layer of muscle. Clint's fists bounced off, as if he was trying to chop down a tree with his bare hands.

Evander absorbed the punches and calmly waited for an opening. Once he saw Clint move in the right direction, he sent a straight punch toward Clint's face. He narrowly missed, but was already following up with his gun hand.

The fist sailed past Clint's head, making a sound like a log being swung at him. As much as he hated to stay in range of Evander's fists, Clint knew he would rather take a punch than make it easy for Evander to shoot him.

The big man's pistol was too close for Evander to waste a shot, so Evander decided to use it as a club instead. Although Clint was quick enough to duck under the swing, he wasn't able to roll to the side fast enough to avoid Evander's sudden downward chop.

Clint gritted his teeth as the gun's handle slammed against his shoulder. Pain raked down through his torso and sent icy tendrils all the way down to his knees. Somehow, Clint remained on his feet.

Beside Clint, John was tussling with another of the guards. He seemed to be having a bit more luck, since he outweighed his man by at least thirty pounds. Although he caught a few punches, John managed to break the gunman's jaw with a well-placed punch. Taking the other man's gun away after that wasn't too difficult.

Clint had both hands wrapped around Evander's wrist and was trying to get the bigger man to let go of his gun. Trying, but not succeeding.

No matter how much muscle Clint put behind his punches, twists or pulls, he always seemed to fall short. Now, Evander was even starting to grin at the strain on Clint's face.

"Give it up, asshole," Evander said as he reached out with his free hand to palm Clint's face. "The three of you don't have what it takes to make a dent in this town."

Clint could feel the gun coming loose. It was only a matter of time before he pried it free. The only question was whether or not he could make it through the next couple of seconds. With Evander's palm pressed against Clint's mouth and his fingers pinching Clint's nose shut, the process of breathing was becoming very difficult.

What little air he'd managed to suck in was almost gone, leaving Clint's lungs aching and the rest of his body reacting to an instinctual panic.

As if to take away the last bit of Clint's hope, Evander pulled his gun free of Clint's hands. "Say good-night, little man," Evander growled as he turned the gun toward Clint's temple.

Watching that barrel from between Evander's fingers made every second drag through Clint's mind. His strength was seeping out of him and the sounds of the gunfight surrounding him had already begun to fade. When he shifted his eyes, Clint felt like they were becoming too big for their sockets. Between that and the fog that had crept into his brain, he couldn't be certain whether or not that truly was someone coming up to Evander's left.

There was a thunderous roar, followed by a flash of light. After that, Clint dropped to one knee and he pulled in a deep, glorious breath. When he blinked away the spots, he saw John standing over Evander, holding a shotgun he must have taken from one of the other gunmen.

"Are you all right?" John asked.

Before Clint could answer, one of the many bullets hissing through the air drilled into the side of John's head.

FORTY-THREE

For a moment, Clint thought that John was going to be all right. After his head had twitched to one side, there was only a slight trickle of blood from his ear. Then, once John's eyes glazed over and he let out a long, gasping breath, Clint knew he was gone.

Clint's first instinct was to see who'd shot John. He quickly knew that search would be futile. Everyone was shooting at everyone else. It was a wonder that Clint was still alive to see it.

"Clint!"

Looking toward the sound of his name, Clint felt more of his senses returning as he pulled in more full breaths. He would have had to be blind to miss Tara as she came rushing toward him wearing that fancy dress.

"Clint, are you hurt?" she asked.

Before he could reply, he saw one of the other gunmen in the street turn toward them. All he could do in the time he had was flatten himself against the ground and bring Tara along with him.

More gunshots filled the air, adding another layer of rings inside of Clint's ears. When he was able to see through the smoke and dust, he sure as hell didn't like what he saw.

"Get out of here, Tara," Clint said. "There's more men coming out of the saloon."

Without even looking in that direction, she stuck close to Clint. "We can't leave! Not without Zack's book."

"Book? What book?"

"The one we—" She was cut off as Clint grabbed her by the waist and pulled her on top of him. He then rolled her over to the other side as a fresh mound of dirt was kicked up in the spot where she'd been.

"Where's Ed?" Clint asked.

"He probably went in for that book! We can't leave him!"

"And we can't stay here for much longer. This place is turning into a battlefield!" Just then, Clint felt something brush against his boot.

It was Evander. The big man's arm was twitching and he began to push himself upright. Although he sported a bloody wound from the shotgun's blast, it was a series of smaller gashes put there by lead pellets at the end of their spread. If Tara had only been a little closer, she might have blown a hole through Evander's chest.

The moment Evander's hand found his gun, he closed his fist around it and looked for a target. Clint was the first man in his sights.

"Here!"

Since he saw something flying at him out of the corner of his eye, Clint reflexively shifted his eyes toward the sound of that desperate voice. The voice was Vernon's and the object flying toward Clint was his modified Colt.

Clint snatched the Colt from the air and pulled the trigger almost immediately. It wasn't his first choice to trust that the gun was loaded, but it was the only one he had. When the Colt bucked against Clint's hand and a gout of flame shot from its barrel, he was half relieved and half surprised.

The shot had been taken so quickly that it didn't do more than make Evander flinch at the sound. That was enough to throw off his aim as he pulled his own trigger. His bullet whipped more than a foot over Clint's head.

But Clint wasn't about to stand by and let Evander adjust his aim. Instead, he pulled his trigger three more times in quick succession, sending a lethal barrage from the Colt, which caught Evander twice in the chest and once in the neck.

Even with the fresh, gaping holes in him, Evander still struggled to take another shot at Clint. It wasn't until he caught one last round through his forehead that Evander slumped forward and died.

Clint's breaths were coming in quick gasps. His blood was pumping so fast that he still felt a little light-headed. He didn't even realize he was reloading the Colt until he snapped the cylinder shut. Taking in his surroundings, Clint found a thick layer of smoke hanging in the air and plenty of bodies scattered upon the ground.

"Where's Ed?" Clint asked.

Tara stood up and looked around in shock. "He got hit. Last I saw him, he was—"

"I'm still here," came a familiar, snarling voice. "Alive and kicking. Well, alive, anyway." Ed pulled himself up, using a hitching post in front of the Number Four. One horse was doing his best to get free of the post, to which the carcasses of another two less fortunate animals were still tied.

Ed had a bloody hole in his left hip, but still managed to get himself upright. "A few more tried to come rushing out here," he said. "But I managed to discourage them. How about you three?"

"I'm . . ." As he started to talk, Clint felt a pinching in his shoulder, arm and side. Those were places he'd either caught glancing shots or Evander's punches. "I'm fine." With that, Clint couldn't help but look down to where John was lying. Tara was already kneeling by the body.

"Oh, no," Ed said as he spotted his partner. He started to get over to John, but could already see the terrible wound in John's head. Ed lowered himself down onto the steps leading to the Number Four and shook his head. "Dammit!"

Gritting his teeth, Clint shifted his eyes toward the saloon. Several faces peered out from the windows, but none of them seemed the least bit interested in coming outside. That being the case, Clint holstered his Colt and started walking toward the door.

"What are you doing?" Tara asked. "There's got to be more of them in there!"

"There's still a job to do. We've come too far and lost too much to ignore that now."

Before Clint could make it to the door, it swung open and a wild-eyed man bolted outside.

"What the hell have you done to my men?"

"Ah," Clint said as he fixed his eyes upon Zack Richards. "Just the man I wanted to see."

FORTY-FOUR

As Zack looked around at all of his fallen men, his eyes became wider and wilder. His lips slowly parted into a vicious snarl and a savage growl churned at the back of his throat. "What is this?" he snarled. "Who the fuck are you?!"

"Tell him who we are, Tara," Clint said warily.

Despite the frilly dress she wore, Tara stepped forward with her shotgun in hand. "Zack Richards, by the order of the United States marshals, you are under arrest."

"This is an outrage!"

"Are you Zack Richards?" Clint asked.

"Yes, but—"

"Then you heard the lady. You're under arrest."

Unable to form a coherent sentence through the rage that flamed up inside of him, Zack looked over to the man standing beside him. Beakman wasn't doing any better. Since he'd spotted Evander's body, Beakman had turned as pale as a ghost.

Zack had spotted someone else as well. "Vernon! You shoot this man in front of me and you can name your reward. I'll take you all the way to the top, right next to me."

Huddled in the gutter across the street, Vernon shook his head. When he spoke, his voice carried through the smoky air just enough to be heard. "These law dogs might've wrapped me up and slung me over the back of a horse, but they were always straight with me. You handed me over to be killed, Mister Richards. I've got a better chance as a prisoner."

"Beakman," Zack said in a grave tone. "You carry a gun. Care to move up in the world?"

When Beakman reached for his gun, Ed was right there to cover him. Beakman stared down the barrel of Ed's gun, removed his own pistol from its holster and handed it over. "There's nobody left, Zack," Beakman said. "It's finished."

Zack planted his feet and squared his shoulders. "Fine," he muttered. "I'll show you how a true man settles his business."

Before anyone else could make a move or say a word, Zack drew his pistol and aimed at the hip. It was a movement that was almost too quick to see and caught both Tara and Ed off their guard. Luckily for them, Clint drew and fired just a little bit quicker and pulled the modified Colt's trigger before Zack could take his first shot.

A bullet whipped through the air, ruffled Tara's sleeve and punched a hole through Zack's flesh and bone. Despite the pain that shot through his body, he managed to keep his footing and pull in another few breaths. After a few moments, Zack tried to return fire, but found he couldn't move his arm.

Clint's bullet carved a messy tunnel through the inside of Zack's elbow and shattered the joint on its way out. As a result, Zack couldn't lift his arm or even close his fingers around his gun. As the pistol slid from his grasp, Zack staggered back to lean against the door frame.

"He's all yours, Tara," Clint said as he holstered the Colt and slowly walked over to pick up Zack's gun. "Alive or nothing, right?"

Tara took the manacles Ed handed to her and nodded. "That's right."

"Now, what were you saying about a book?"

"It's inside. Zack was writing in it as he was talking over something regarding a group of federal judges."

"Judges!" Zack shouted. "I'm a judge! You'll hang for this, Adams! You can't shoot a judge. Isn't that right, Beakman?"

Clint looked over to the man in the black suit.

"That book has some items in there," Beakman said in a defeated tone. "I kept records of my own. Every politician or lawman that took a bribe from us is in there. I'll hand them over if you arrange to give me a pardon for my part in all this."

Senator Grinbee had emerged from his own hiding spot by then and was mounted up on his own horse. "What about those assassins waiting to kill my fellow senators or judges if they failed to follow that maniac's orders?"

Beakman shook his head in disgust. "If the U.S. marshals can't round them up after seeing what I give them and listening to what I say, they don't deserve to wear their badges."

"Tara will go with you to collect those documents," Clint said. "I'm sure she will see what she can do about the rest." Clint looked around at all the people who'd gathered in the saloon, as well as in the streets, to look at the bloody mess that lay in front of the Number Four.

"What about the rest of you?" Clint asked. "Anyone else want to stand and fight for this man?"

There were no takers.

"Looks like you lost your grip on Harbinger, Zack," Clint said. "Something tells me the rest of what you thought you'd made won't be far behind."

"I'm a judge, you son of a bitch," Zack spat in a voice that got faster and more venomous with every word. "You can't do this to me! I'm the man that pulls the strings for this whole goddamn country! I'm the one that makes all the decisions! I decide who lives and who dies! Not you. Not anyone else. ME!"

Ed kept his gun trained on Beakman and Vernon, but both of those prisoners were following him of their own free will. And they weren't the only ones to lose interest in Zack Richards. Those who'd been watching the fight now scuttled off to do their own business.

A few minutes later, the streets were clear, apart from Clint and Tara. They were in their saddles and waiting for Ed to come back.

"I feel like a fool for siding with that lunatic," Vernon said as he glanced over at Zack. Clint held the reins of the horse they'd found for Vernon. Although he wasn't tied up like an inchworm, his wrists and ankles were bound and tied to his saddle. "Still, I gotta admit, it does me good to see him wrapped up like that."

Clint reached back to pat Zack on the shoulder. This time, it was Richards who was bound from shoulders to knees in rope and slung over Eclipse's back. "Yeah. Me too."

His eyes went to another bundle on the back of Ed's horse. John's body had been wrapped in cloth and placed there so his partner could bring him home.

Just then, Tara walked out with Beakman held at gunpoint in front of her. She carried a leather satchel under her arm. "Zack's book is in here, along with plenty of others. Looks like there's even the forged papers that he was talking about. I doubt he'll get any professional courtesy from any judge in this country."

"You did a hell of a job, Adams," Ed said. "I wouldn't be surprised if Tucker offered you a job."

Despite the smile that came onto Tara's face when she heard that, Clint shrugged and steered Eclipse toward the edge of town. "I'll have to burn that bridge when I come to it. Right now, I'm more concerned about getting out of here. I've had my fill of this town."

Judging by the looks on everyone's faces, even the prisoners were more than happy to follow him.

Watch for

THE ROAD TO HELL

293rd novel in the exciting GUNSMITH series
from Jove

Coming in May!

GIANT ACTION! GIANT ADVENTURE!

THE GUNSMITH

GIANT

GIANT WESTERNS FEATURING THE GUNSMITH

THE GHOST OF BILLY THE KID
0-515-13622-0

LITTLE SURESHOT AND THE WILD WEST SHOW
0-515-13851-7

DEAD WEIGHT
0-515-14028-7

J799

J. R. ROBERTS

THE GUNSMITH

Explore the exciting Old West with one of the men who made it wild!

AVAILABLE WHEREVER BOOKS ARE SOLD OR AT PENGUIN.COM

(Ad # B112)